INVISIBLE CITIES

Italo Calvino was born in Cuba in 1923, and grew up in Italy. He was an essayist and journalist and a member of the editorial staff of Einaudi in Turin. His books include *Marcovaldo, Invisible Cities, The Castle of Crossed Destinies, If on a winter's night a traveller* and *Mr Palomar*. In 1973 he won the prestigious Premio Feltrinelli. He died in 1985.

BY ITALO CALVINO

Italo Calvino

INVISIBLE CITIES

TRANSLATED FROM THE ITALIAN BY
William Weaver

VINTAGE

Published by Vintage 1997

8 10 9

First published in Italy as *Le cita invisibili*
Copyright © Giulio Einaudi editore, s.p.a. 1972
English translation copyright
© Harcourt Brace Jovanovich, Inc. 1974

First published in Great Britain by
Secker & Warburg Ltd, 1974

Vintage
The Random House Group Limited,
20 Vauxhall Bridge Road, London SW1V 2SA

Random House Australia (Pty) Limited
20 Alfred Street, Milsons Point, Sydney
New South Wales 2061, Australia

Random House New Zealand Limited
18 Poland Road, Glenfield
Auckland 10, New Zealand

Random House (Pty) Limited
Endulini, 5a Jubilee Road, Parktown 2193, South Africa

The Random House Group Limited Reg. No. 954009

www.randomhouse.co.uk

A CIP catalogue record for this book
is available from the British Library

ISBN 0 7493 9764 0

Papers used by Random House are natural, recyclable
products made from wood grown in sustainable forests.
The manufacturing processes conform to the environ-
mental regulations of the country of origin

Printed and bound in Great Britain by
Cox & Wyman Ltd, Reading, Berkshire

Contents

3

4

5

6

7

8

9

Italo Calvino

INVISIBLE CITIES

1

*Kublai Khan does not necessarily believe everything Marco
Polo says when he describes the cities visited on his expeditions, but the emperor of the Tartars does continue listening
to the young Venetian with greater attention and curiosity
than he shows any other messenger or explorer of his. In the
lives of emperors there is a moment which follows pride in
the boundless extension of the territories we have conquered,
and the melancholy and relief of knowing we shall soon
give up any thought of knowing and understanding them.
There is a sense of emptiness that comes over us at evening,
with the odor of the elephants after the rain and the san-
dalwood ashes growing cold in the braziers, a dizziness that
makes rivers and mountains tremble on the fallow curves of
the planispheres where they are portrayed, and rolls up, one
after the other, the despatches announcing to us the collapse
of the last enemy troops, from defeat to defeat, and flakes
the wax of the seals of obscure kings who beseech our
armies' protection, offering in exchange annual tributes of
precious metals, tanned hides, and tortoise shell. It is the
desperate moment when we discover that this empire, which
had seemed to us the sum of all wonders, is an endless,
formless ruin, that corruption's gangrene has spread too far
to be healed by our scepter, that the triumph over enemy
sovereigns has made us the heirs of their long undoing.
Only in Marco Polo's accounts was Kublai Khan able to*

discern, through the walls and towers destined to crumble, the tracery of a pattern so subtle it could escape the termites' gnawing.

Cities & Memory · 1

Leaving there and proceeding for three days toward the east, you reach Diomira, a city with sixty silver domes, bronze statues of all the gods, streets paved with lead, a crystal theater, a golden cock that crows each morning on a tower. All these beauties will already be familiar to the visitor, who has seen them also in other cities. But the special quality of this city for the man who arrives there on a September evening, when the days are growing shorter and the multicolored lamps are lighted all at once at the doors of the food stalls and from a terrace a woman's voice cries ooh!, is that he feels envy toward those who now believe they have once before lived an evening identical to this and who think they were happy, that time.

Cities & Memory · 2

When a man rides a long time through wild regions he feels the desire for a city. Finally he comes to Isidora, a city where the buildings have spiral staircases encrusted with spiral seashells, where perfect telescopes and violins are made, where the foreigner hesitating between two women always encounters a third, where cockfights degenerate into bloody brawls among the bettors. He was thinking of all these things when he desired a city. Isidora, therefore, is the city of his dreams: with one difference. The dreamed-of city contained him as a young man; he arrives at Isidora in his old age. In the square there is the wall where the old men sit and watch the young go by; he is seated in a row with them. Desires are already memories.

Cities & Desire · 1

There are two ways of describing the city of Dorothea: you can say that four aluminum towers rise from its walls flanking seven gates with spring-operated drawbridges that span the moat whose water feeds four green canals which cross the city, dividing it into nine quarters, each with three hundred houses and seven hundred chimneys. And bearing in mind that the nubile girls of each quarter marry youths of other quarters and their parents exchange the goods that each family holds in monopoly—bergamot, sturgeon roe, astrolabes, amethysts—you can then work from these facts until you learn everything you wish about the city in the past, present, and future. Or else you can say, like the camel driver who took me there: "I arrived here in my first youth, one morning, many people were hurrying along the streets toward the market, the women had fine teeth and looked you straight in the eye, three soldiers on a platform played the trumpet, and all around wheels turned and colored banners fluttered in the wind. Before then I had known only the desert and the caravan routes. In the years that followed, my eyes returned to contemplate the desert expanses and the caravan routes; but now I know this path is only one of the many that opened before me on that morning in Dorothea."

Cities & Memory · 3

In vain, great-hearted Kublai, shall I attempt to describe Zaira, city of high bastions. I could tell you how many steps make up the streets rising like stairways, and the degree of the arcades' curves, and what kind of zinc scales cover the roofs; but I already know this would be the same as telling you nothing. The city does not consist of this, but of relationships between the measurements of its space and the events of its past: the height of a lamppost and the distance from the ground of a hanged usurper's swaying feet; the line strung from the lamppost to the railing opposite and the festoons that decorate the course of the queen's nuptial procession; the height of that railing and the leap of the adulterer who climbed over it at dawn; the tilt of a guttering and a cat's progress along it as he slips into the same window; the firing range of a gunboat which has suddenly appeared beyond the cape and the bomb that destroys the guttering; the rips in the fish net and the three old men seated on the dock mending nets and telling each other for the hundredth time the story of the gunboat of the usurper, who some say was the queen's illegitimate son, abandoned in his swaddling clothes there on the dock.

As this wave from memories flows in, the city soaks it up like a sponge and expands. A description of Zaira as it is today should contain all Zaira's past.

The city, however, does not tell its past, but contains it like the lines of a hand, written in the corners of the streets, the gratings of the windows, the banisters of the steps, the antennae of the lightning rods, the poles of the flags, every segment marked in turn with scratches, indentations, scrolls.

Cities & Desire · 2

At the end of three days, moving southward, you come upon Anastasia, a city with concentric canals watering it and kites flying over it. I should now list the wares that can profitably be bought here: agate, onyx, chrysoprase, and other varieties of chalcedony; I should praise the flesh of the golden pheasant cooked here over fires of seasoned cherry wood and sprinkled with much sweet marjoram; and tell of the women I have seen bathing in the pool of a garden and who sometimes—it is said—invite the stranger to disrobe with them and chase them in the water. But with all this, I would not be telling you the city's true essence; for while the description of Anastasia awakens desires one at a time only to force you to stifle them, when you are in the heart of Anastasia one morning your desires waken all at once and surround you. The city appears to you as a whole where no desire is lost and of which you are a part, and since it enjoys everything you do not enjoy, you can do nothing but inhabit this desire and be content. Such is the power, sometimes called malignant, sometimes benign, that Anastasia, the treacherous city, possesses; if for eight hours a day you work as a cutter of agate, onyx, chrysoprase, your labor which gives form to desire takes from desire its form, and you believe you are enjoying Anastasia wholly when you are only its slave.

Cities & Signs · 1

You walk for days among trees and among stones. Rarely does the eye light on a thing, and then only when it has recognized that thing as the sign of another thing: a print in the sand indicates the tiger's passage; a marsh announces a vein of water; the hibiscus flower, the end of winter. All the rest is silent and interchangeable; trees and stones are only what they are.

Finally the journey leads to the city of Tamara. You penetrate it along streets thick with signboards jutting from the walls. The eye does not see things but images of things that mean other things: pincers point out the tooth-drawer's house; a tankard, the tavern; halberds, the barracks; scales, the grocer's. Statues and shields depict lions, dolphins, towers, stars: a sign that something—who knows what?—has as its sign a lion or a dolphin or a tower or a star. Other signals warn of what is forbidden in a given place (to enter the alley with wagons, to urinate behind the kiosk, to fish with your pole from the bridge) and what is allowed (watering zebras, playing bowls, burning relatives' corpses). From the doors of the temples the gods' statues are seen, each portrayed with his attributes—the cornucopia, the hourglass, the medusa—so that the worshiper can recognize them and address his prayers correctly. If a building has no signboard or figure, its very form and the position it occupies in the city's order suffice to indicate its function: the palace, the prison, the mint, the Pythagorean school, the brothel. The wares, too, which the vendors display on their stalls are valuable not in themselves but as signs of other things: the embroidered headband stands for elegance; the gilded palanquin, power; the volumes of Averroes, learning; the ankle bracelet, voluptuousness. Your gaze scans the streets as if they were written pages: the city says everything you must think, makes you repeat her discourse, and while you believe you are visiting Tamara you are only recording the names with which she defines herself and all her parts.

However the city may really be, beneath this thick coating of signs, whatever it may contain or conceal, you leave Tamara without having discovered it. Outside, the land stretches, empty, to the horizon; the sky opens, with speeding clouds. In the shape that chance and wind give the clouds, you are already intent on recognizing figures: a sailing ship, a hand, an elephant. . . .

Cities & Memory · 4

Beyond six rivers and three mountain ranges rises Zora, a city that no one, having seen it, can forget. But not because, like other memorable cities, it leaves an unusual image in your recollections. Zora has the quality of remaining in your memory point by point, in its succession of streets, of houses along the streets, and of doors and windows in the houses, though nothing in them possesses a special beauty or rarity. Zora's secret lies in the way your gaze runs over patterns following one another as in a musical score where not a note can be altered or displaced. The man who knows by heart how Zora is made, if he is unable to sleep at night, can imagine he is walking along the streets and he remembers the order by which the copper clock follows the barber's striped awning, then the fountain with the nine jets, the astronomer's glass tower, the melon vendor's kiosk, the statue of the hermit and the lion, the Turkish bath, the café at the corner, the alley that leads to the harbor. This city which cannot be expunged from the mind is like an armature, a honeycomb in whose cells each of us can place the things he wants to remember: names of famous men, virtues, numbers, vegetable and mineral classifications, dates of battles, constellations, parts of speech. Between each idea and each point of the itinerary an affinity or a contrast can be established, serving as an immediate aid to memory. So the world's most learned men are those who have memorized Zora.

But in vain I set out to visit the city: forced to remain motionless and always the same, in order to be more easily remembered, Zora has languished, disintegrated, disappeared. The earth has forgotten her.

Cities & Desire · 3

Despina can be reached in two ways: by ship or by camel. The city displays one face to the traveler arriving overland and a different one to him who arrives by sea.

When the camel driver sees, at the horizon of the tableland, the pinnacles of the skyscrapers come into view, the radar antennae, the white and red windsocks flapping, the chimneys belching smoke, he thinks of a ship; he knows it is a city, but he thinks of it as a vessel that will take him away from the desert, a windjammer about to cast off, with the breeze already swelling the sails, not yet unfurled, or a steamboat with its boiler vibrating in the iron keel; and he thinks of all the ports, the foreign merchandise the cranes unload on the docks, the taverns where crews of different flags break bottles over one another's heads, the lighted, ground-floor windows, each with a woman combing her hair.

In the coastline's haze, the sailor discerns the form of a camel's withers, an embroidered saddle with glittering fringe between two spotted humps, advancing and swaying; he knows it is a city, but he thinks of it as a camel from whose pack hang wineskins and bags of candied fruit, date wine, tobacco leaves, and already he sees himself at the head of a long caravan taking him away from the desert of the sea, toward oases of fresh water in the palm trees' jagged shade, toward palaces of thick, whitewashed walls, tiled courts where girls are dancing barefoot, moving their arms, half-hidden by their veils, and half-revealed.

Each city receives its form from the desert it opposes; and so the camel driver and the sailor see Despina, a border city between two deserts.

Cities & Signs · 2

Travelers return from the city of Zirma with distinct memories: a blind black man shouting in the crowd, a lunatic teetering on a skyscraper's cornice, a girl walking with a puma on a leash. Actually many of the blind men who tap their canes on Zirma's cobblestones are black; in every skyscraper there is someone going mad; all lunatics spend hours on cornices; there is no puma that some girl does not raise, as a whim. The city is redundant: it repeats itself so that something will stick in the mind.

I too am returning from Zirma: my memory includes dirigibles flying in all directions, at window level; streets of shops where tattoos are drawn on sailors' skin; underground trains crammed with obese women suffering from the humidity. My traveling companions, on the other hand, swear they saw only one dirigible hovering among the city's spires, only one tattoo artist arranging needles and inks and pierced patterns on his bench, only one fat woman fanning herself on a train's platform. Memory is redundant: it repeats signs so that the city can begin to exist.

Thin Cities · 1

Isaura, city of the thousand wells, is said to rise over a deep, subterranean lake. On all sides, wherever the inhabitants dig long vertical holes in the ground, they succeed in drawing up water, as far as the city extends, and no farther. Its green border repeats the dark outline of the buried lake; an invisible landscape conditions the visible one; everything that moves in the sunlight is driven by the lapping wave enclosed beneath the rock's calcareous sky.

Consequently two forms of religion exist in Isaura.

The city's gods, according to some people, live in the depths, in the black lake that feeds the underground streams. According to others, the gods live in the buckets that rise, suspended from a cable, as they appear over the edge of the wells, in the revolving pulleys, in the windlasses of the norias, in the pump handles, in the blades of the windmills that draw the water up from the drillings, in the trestles that support the twisting probes, in the reservoirs perched on stilts over the roofs, in the slender arches of the aqueducts, in all the columns of water, the vertical pipes, the plungers, the drains, all the way up to the weathercocks that surmount the airy scaffoldings of Isaura, a city that moves entirely upward.

Sent off to inspect the remote provinces, the Great Khan's envoys and tax-collectors duly returned to Kai-ping-fu and to the gardens of magnolias in whose shade Kublai strolled, listening to their long reports. The ambassadors were Persians, Armenians, Syrians, Copts, Turkomans; the emperor is he who is a foreigner to each of his subjects, and only through foreign eyes and ears could the empire manifest its existence to Kublai. In languages incomprehensible to the Khan, the envoys related information heard in languages incomprehensible to them: from this opaque, dense stridor emerged the revenues received by the imperial treasury, the first and last names of officials dismissed and decapitated, the dimensions of the canals that the narrow rivers fed in times of drought. But when the young Venetian made his report, a different communication was established between him and the emperor. Newly arrived and totally ignorant of the Levantine languages, Marco Polo could express himself only with gestures, leaps, cries of wonder and of horror, animal barkings or hootings, or with objects he took from his knapsacks—ostrich plumes, pea-shooters, quartzes—which he arranged in front of him like chessmen. Returning from the missions on which Kublai sent him, the ingenious foreigner improvised pantomimes that the sovereign had to interpret: one city was depicted by the leap of a fish escaping the cormorant's beak to fall into a net; another city by a naked man running through fire unscorched; a third by a skull, its teeth green with mold, clenching a round, white pearl. The Great Khan deciphered the signs, but the connection between them and the places visited remained uncertain; he never knew whether Marco wished to enact an adventure that had befallen him on his journey, an exploit of the city's founder, the prophecy of an astrologer, a rebus or a charade to indicate a name. But, obscure or obvious as it might be, everything Marco displayed had the power of emblems, which, once seen, cannot be forgotten or confused. In the Khan's mind the empire was reflected in a desert of labile and interchangeable data, like grains of sand, from which there appeared, for each city and province, the figures evoked by the Venetian's logographs.

As the seasons passed and his missions continued, Marco mastered the Tartar language and the national idioms and tribal dialects. Now his accounts were the most precise and detailed that the Great Khan could wish and there was no question or curiosity which they did not satisfy. And yet each piece of information about a place recalled to the emperor's mind that first gesture or object with which Marco had designated the place. The new fact received a meaning from that emblem and also added to the emblem a new meaning. Perhaps, Kublai thought, the empire is nothing but a zodiac of the mind's phantasms.

"On the day when I know all the emblems," he asked

Marco, "shall I be able to possess my empire, at last?"

And the Venetian answered: "Sire, do not believe it. On that day you will be an emblem among emblems."

2

"The other ambassadors warn me of famines, extortions, conspiracies, or else they inform me of newly discovered turquoise mines, advantageous prices in marten furs, suggestions for supplying damascened blades. And you?" the Great Khan asked Polo, "you return from lands equally distant and you can tell me only the thoughts that come to a man who sits on his doorstep at evening to enjoy the cool air. What is the use, then, of all your traveling?"

"It is evening. We are seated on the steps of your palace. There is a slight breeze," Marco Polo answered. "Whatever country my words may evoke around you, you will see it from such a vantage point, even if instead of the palace there is a village on pilings and the breeze carries the stench of a muddy estuary."

"My gaze is that of a man meditating, lost in thought— I admit it. But yours? You cross archipelagoes, tundras, mountain ranges. You would do as well never moving from here."

The Venetian knew that when Kublai became vexed with him, the emperor wanted to follow more clearly a private train of thought; so Marco's answers and objections took their place in a discourse already proceeding on its own, in the Great Khan's head. That is to say, between the two of them it did not matter whether questions and solutions were uttered aloud or whether each of the two went on pondering in silence. In fact, they were silent,

27

their eyes half-closed. reclining on cushions. swaying in hammocks. smoking long amber pipes.

Marco Polo imagined answering (or Kublai Khan imagined his answer) that the more one was lost in unfamiliar quarters of distant cities. the more one understood the other cities he had crossed to arrive there; and he retraced the stages of his journeys. and he came to know the port from which he had set sail. and the familiar places of his youth. and the surroundings of home. and a little square of Venice where he gamboled as a child.

At this point Kublai Khan interrupted him or imagined interrupting him, or Marco Polo imagined himself interrupted. with a question such as: "You advance always with your head turned back?" or "Is what you see always behind you?" or rather. "Does your journey take place only in the past?"

All this so that Marco Polo could explain or imagine explaining or be imagined explaining or succeed finally in explaining to himself that what he sought was always something lying ahead. and even if it was a matter of the past it was a past that changed gradually as he advanced on his journey, because the traveler's past changes according to the route he has followed: not the immediate past. that is, to which each day that goes by adds a day, but the more remote past. Arriving at each new city, the traveler finds again a past of his that he did not know he had: *the foreignness of what you no longer are or no longer possess lies in wait for you in foreign, unpossessed places.*

Marco enters a city; he sees someone in a square living a life or an instant that could be his; he could now be in that man's place, if he had stopped in time, long ago; or if, long ago, at a crossroads, instead of taking one road he had taken the opposite one, and after long wandering he had come to be in the place of that man in that square. By now, from that real or hypothetical past of his, he is excluded; he cannot stop; he must go on to another city, where another of his pasts awaits him, or something perhaps that had been a possible future of his and is now someone else's present. Futures not achieved are only branches of the past: dead branches.

"Journeys to relive your past?" was the Khan's question at this point, a question which could also have been formulated: "Journeys to recover your future?"

And Marco's answer was: "Elsewhere is a negative mirror. The traveler recognizes the little that is his, discovering the much he has not had and will never have."

Cities & Memory · 5

In Maurilia, the traveler is invited to visit the city and, at the same time, to examine some old post cards that show it as it used to be: the same identical square with a hen in the place of the bus station, a bandstand in the place of the overpass, two young ladies with white parasols in the place of the munitions factory. If the traveler does not wish to disappoint the inhabitants, he must praise the post-card city and prefer it to the present one, though he must be careful to contain his regret at the changes within definite limits: admitting that the magnificence and prosperity of the metropolis Maurilia, when compared to the old, provincial Maurilia, cannot compensate for a certain lost grace, which, however, can be appreciated only now in the old post cards, whereas before, when that provincial Maurilia was before one's eyes, one saw absolutely nothing graceful and would see it even less today, if Maurilia had remained unchanged; and in any case the metropolis has the added attraction that, through what it has become, one can look back with nostalgia at what it was.

Beware of saying to them that sometimes different cities follow one another on the same site and under the same name, born and dying without knowing one another, without communication among themselves. At times even the names of the inhabitants remain the same, and their voices' accent, and also the features of the faces; but the gods who live beneath names and above places have gone off without a word and outsiders have settled in their place. It is pointless to ask whether the new ones are better or worse than the old, since there is no connection between them, just as the old post cards do not depict Maurilia as it was, but a different city which, by chance, was called Maurilia, like this one.

Cities & Desire · 4

In the center of Fedora, that gray stone metropolis, stands a metal building with a crystal globe in every room. Looking into each globe, you see a blue city, the model of a different Fedora. These are the forms the city could have taken if, for one reason or another, it had not become what we see today. In every age someone, looking at Fedora as it was, imagined a way of making it the ideal city, but while he constructed his miniature model, Fedora was already no longer the same as before, and what had been until yesterday a possible future became only a toy in a glass globe.

The building with the globes is now Fedora's museum: every inhabitant visits it, chooses the city that corresponds to his desires, contemplates it, imagining his reflection in the medusa pond that would have collected the waters of the canal (if it had not been dried up), the view from the high canopied box along the avenue reserved for elephants (now banished from the city), the fun of sliding down the spiral, twisting minaret (which never found a pedestal from which to rise).

On the map of your empire, O Great Khan, there must be room both for the big, stone Fedora and the little Fedoras in glass globes. Not because they are all equally real, but because all are only assumptions.

The one contains what is accepted as necessary when it is not yet so; the others, what is imagined as possible and, a moment later, is possible no longer.

Cities & Signs · 3

The man who is traveling and does not yet know the city awaiting him along his route wonders what the palace will be like, the barracks, the mill, the theater, the bazaar. In every city of the empire every building is different and set in a different order: but as soon as the stranger arrives at the unknown city and his eye penetrates the pine cone of pagodas and garrets and haymows, following the scrawl of canals, gardens, rubbish heaps, he immediately distinguishes which are the princes' palaces, the high priests' temples, the tavern, the prison, the slum. This—some say—confirms the hypothesis that each man bears in his mind a city made only of differences, a city without figures and without form, and the individual cities fill it up.

This is not true of Zoe. In every point of this city you can, in turn, sleep, make tools, cook, accumulate gold, disrobe, reign, sell, question oracles. Any one of its pyramid roofs could cover the leprosarium or the odalisques' baths. The traveler roams all around and has nothing but doubts: he is unable to distinguish the features of the city, the features he keeps distinct in his mind also mingle. He infers this: if existence in all its moments is all of itself, Zoe is the place of indivisible existence. But why, then, does the city exist? What line separates the inside from the outside, the rumble of wheels from the howl of wolves?

Thin Cities · 2

Now I shall tell of the city of Zenobia, which is wonderful in this fashion: though set on dry terrain it stands on high pilings, and the houses are of bamboo and zinc, with many platforms and balconies placed on stilts at various heights, crossing one another, linked by ladders and hanging sidewalks, surmounted by cone-roofed belvederes, barrels storing water, weather vanes, jutting pulleys, and fish poles, and cranes.

No one remembers what need or command or desire drove Zenobia's founders to give their city this form, and so there is no telling whether it was satisfied by the city as we see it today, which has perhaps grown through successive superimpositions from the first, now undecipherable plan. But what is certain is that if you ask an inhabitant of Zenobia to describe his vision of a happy life, it is always a city like Zenobia that he imagines, with its pilings and its suspended stairways, a Zenobia perhaps quite different, a-flutter with banners and ribbons, but always derived by combining elements of that first model.

This said, it is pointless trying to decide whether Zenobia is to be classified among happy cities or among the unhappy. It makes no sense to divide cities into these two species, but rather into another two: those that through the years and the changes continue to give their form to desires, and those in which desires either erase the city or are erased by it.

Trading Cities · 1

Proceeding eighty miles into the northwest wind, you reach the city of Euphemia, where the merchants of seven nations gather at every solstice and equinox. The boat that lands there with a cargo of ginger and cotton will set sail again, its hold filled with pistachio nuts and poppy seeds, and the caravan that has just unloaded sacks of nutmegs and raisins is already cramming its saddlebags with bolts of golden muslin for the return journey. But what drives men to travel up rivers and cross deserts to come here is not only the exchange of wares, which you could find, everywhere the same, in all the bazaars inside and outside the Great Khan's empire, scattered at your feet on the same yellow mats, in the shade of the same awnings protecting them from the flies, offered with the same lying reduction in prices. You do not come to Euphemia only to buy and sell, but also because at night, by the fires all around the market, seated on sacks or barrels or stretched out on piles of carpets, at each word that one man says—such as "wolf," "sister," "hidden treasure," "battle," "scabies," "lovers"—the others tell, each one, his tale of wolves, sisters, treasures, scabies, lovers, battles. And you know that in the long journey ahead of you, when to keep awake against the camel's swaying or the junk's rocking, you start summoning up your memories one by one, your wolf will have become

another wolf, your sister a different sister, your battle other battles, on your return from Euphemia, the
city where memory is traded at every solstice and at
every equinox.

Newly arrived and quite ignorant of the languages of the Levant, Marco Polo could express himself only by drawing objects from his baggage—drums, salt fish, necklaces of wart hogs' teeth—and pointing to them with gestures, leaps, cries of wonder or of horror, imitating the bay of the jackal, the hoot of the owl.

The connections between one element of the story and another were not always obvious to the emperor; the objects could have various meanings: a quiver filled with arrows could indicate the approach of war, or an abundance of game, or else an armorer's shop; an hourglass could mean time passing, or time past, or sand, or a place where hourglasses are made.

But what enhanced for Kublai every event or piece of news reported by his inarticulate informer was the space that remained around it, a void not filled with words. The descriptions of cities Marco Polo visited had this virtue: you could wander through them in thought, become lost, stop and enjoy the cool air, or run off.

As time went by, words began to replace objects and gestures in Marco's tales: first exclamations, isolated nouns, dry verbs, then phrases, ramified and leafy discourses, metaphors and tropes. The foreigner had learned to speak the emperor's language or the emperor to understand the language of the foreigner.

But you would have said communication between them

was less happy than in the past: to be sure, words were more useful than objects and gestures in listing the most important things of every province and city—monuments, markets, costumes, fauna and flora—and yet when Polo began to talk about how life must be in those places, day after day, evening after evening, words failed him, and little by little, he went back to relying on gestures, grimaces, glances.

So, for each city, after the fundamental information given in precise words, he followed with a mute commentary, holding up his hands, palms out, or backs, or sideways, in straight or oblique movements, spasmodic or slow. A new kind of dialogue was established: the Great Khan's white hands, heavy with rings, answered with stately movements the sinewy, agile hands of the merchant. As an understanding grew between them, their hands began to assume fixed attitudes, each of which corresponded to a shift of mood, in their alternation and repetition. And as the vocabulary of things was renewed with new samples of merchandise, the repertory of mute comment tended to become closed, stable. The pleasure of falling back on it also diminished in both; in their conversations, most of the time, they remained silent and immobile.

3

Kublai Khan had noticed that Marco Polo's cities resembled one another, as if the passage from one to another involved not a journey but a change of elements. Now, from each city Marco described to him, the Great Khan's mind set out on its own, and after dismantling the city piece by piece, he reconstructed it in other ways, substituting components, shifting them, inverting them.

Marco, meanwhile, continued reporting his journey, but the emperor was no longer listening.

Kublai interrupted him: "From now on I shall describe the cities and you will tell me if they exist and are as I have conceived them. I shall begin by asking you about a city of stairs, exposed to the sirocco, on a half-moon bay. Now I shall list some of the wonders it contains: a glass tank high as a cathedral so people can follow the swimming and flying of the swallow fish and draw auguries from them; a palm tree which plays the harp with its fronds in the wind; a square with a horseshoe marble table around it, a marble tablecloth, set with foods and beverages also of marble."

"Sire, your mind has been wandering. This is precisely the city I was telling you about when you interrupted me."

"You know it? Where is it? What is its name?"

"It has neither name nor place. I shall repeat the reason why I was describing it to you: from the number of imaginable cities we must exclude those whose elements are as-

sembled without a connecting thread, an inner rule, a perspective, a discourse. With cities, it is as with dreams: everything imaginable can be dreamed, but even the most unexpected dream is a rebus that conceals a desire or, its reverse, a fear. Cities, like dreams, are made of desires and fears, even if the thread of their discourse is secret, their rules are absurd, their perspectives deceitful, and everything conceals something else."

"I have neither desires nor fears," the Khan declared, "and my dreams are composed either by my mind or by chance."

"Cities also believe they are the work of the mind or of chance, but neither the one nor the other suffices to hold up their walls. You take delight not in a city's seven or seventy wonders, but in the answer it gives to a question of yours."

"Or the question it asks you, forcing you to answer, like Thebes through the mouth of the Sphinx."

From there, after six days and seven nights, you arrive at Zobeide, the white city, well exposed to the moon, with streets wound about themselves as in a skein. They tell this tale of its foundation: men of various nations had an identical dream. They saw a woman running at night through an unknown city; she was seen from behind, with long hair, and she was naked. They dreamed of pursuing her. As they twisted and turned, each of them lost her. After the dream they set out in search of that city; they never found it, but they found one another; they decided to build a city like the one in the dream. In laying out the streets, each followed the course of his pursuit; at the spot where they had lost the fugitive's trail, they arranged spaces and walls differently from the dream, so she would be unable to escape again.

This was the city of Zobeide, where they settled, waiting for that scene to be repeated one night. None of them, asleep or awake, ever saw the woman again. The city's streets were streets where they went to work every day, with no link any more to the dreamed chase. Which, for that matter, had long been forgotten.

New men arrived from other lands, having had a dream like theirs, and in the city of Zobeide, they recognized something of the streets of the dream, and they changed the positions of arcades and stairways to resemble more closely the path of the pursued woman and so, at the spot where she had vanished, there would remain no avenue of escape.

The first to arrive could not understand what drew these people to Zobeide, this ugly city, this trap.

Cities & Signs · 4

Of all the changes of language a traveler in distant lands must face, none equals that which awaits him in the city of Hypatia, because the change regards not words, but things. I entered Hypatia one morning, a magnolia garden was reflected in blue lagoons, I walked among the hedges, sure I would discover young and beautiful ladies bathing; but at the bottom of the water, crabs were biting the eyes of the suicides, stones tied around their necks, their hair green with seaweed.

I felt cheated and I decided to demand justice of the sultan. I climbed the porphyry steps of the palace with the highest domes, I crossed six tiled courtyards with fountains. The central hall was barred by iron gratings: convicts with black chains on their feet were hauling up basalt blocks from a quarry that opened underground.

I could only question the philosophers. I entered the great library, I became lost among shelves collapsing under the vellum bindings, I followed the alphabetical order of vanished alphabets, up and down halls, stairs, bridges. In the most remote papyrus cabinet, in a cloud of smoke, the dazed eyes of an adolescent appeared to me, as he lay on a mat, his lips glued to an opium pipe.

"Where is the sage?"

The smoker pointed out of the window. It was a

garden with children's games: ninepins, a swing, a top. The philosopher was seated on the lawn. He said: "Signs form a language, but not the one you think you know."

I realized I had to free myself from the images which in the past had announced to me the things I sought: only then would I succeed in understanding the language of Hypatia.

Now I have only to hear the neighing of horses and the cracking of whips and I am seized with amorous trepidation: in Hypatia you have to go to the stables and riding rings to see the beautiful women who mount the saddle, thighs naked, greaves on their calves, and as soon as a young foreigner approaches, they fling him on the piles of hay or sawdust and press their firm nipples against him.

And when my spirit wants no stimulus or nourishment save music, I know it is to be sought in the cemeteries: the musicians hide in the tombs; from grave to grave flute trills, harp chords answer one another.

True, also in Hypatia the day will come when my only desire will be to leave. I know I must not go down to the harbor then, but climb the citadel's highest pinnacle and wait for a ship to go by up there. But will it ever go by? There is no language without deceit.

Thin Cities · 3

Whether Armilla is like this because it is unfinished or because it has been demolished, whether the cause is some enchantment or only a whim, I do not know. The fact remains that it has no walls, no ceilings, no floors: it has nothing that makes it seem a city, except the water pipes that rise vertically where the houses should be and spread out horizontally where the floors should be: a forest of pipes that end in taps, showers, spouts, overflows. Against the sky a lavabo's white stands out, or a bathtub, or some other porcelain, like late fruit still hanging from the boughs. You would think the plumbers had finished their job and gone away before the bricklayers arrived; or else their hydraulic systems, indestructible, had survived a catastrophe, an earthquake, or the corrosion of termites.

Abandoned before or after it was inhabited, Armilla cannot be called deserted. At any hour, raising your eyes among the pipes, you are likely to glimpse a young woman, or many young women, slender, not tall of stature, luxuriating in the bathtubs or arching their backs under the showers suspended in the void, washing or drying or perfuming themselves, or combing their long hair at a mirror. In the sun, the threads of water fanning from the showers glisten, the jets of the taps, the spurts, the splashes, the sponges' suds.

I have come to this explanation: the streams of water channeled in the pipes of Armilla have remained in the possession of nymphs and naiads. Accustomed to traveling along underground veins, they found it easy to enter into the new aquatic realm, to burst from multiple fountains, to find new mirrors, new games, new ways of enjoying the water. Their invasion may have driven out the human beings, or Armilla may have been built by humans as a votive offering to win the favor of the nymphs, offended at the misuse of the waters. In any case, now they seem content, these maidens: in the morning you hear them singing.

Trading Cities · 2

In Chloe, a great city, the people who move through the streets are all strangers. At each encounter, they imagine a thousand things about one another; meetings which could take place between them, conversations, surprises, caresses, bites. But no one greets anyone; eyes lock for a second, then dart away, seeking other eyes, never stopping.

A girl comes along, twirling a parasol on her shoulder, and twirling slightly also her rounded hips. A woman in black comes along, showing her full age, her eyes restless beneath her veil, her lips trembling. A tattooed giant comes along; a young man with white hair; a female dwarf; two girls, twins, dressed in coral. Something runs among them, an exchange of glances like lines that connect one figure with another and draw arrows, stars, triangles, until all combinations are used up in a moment, and other characters come on to the scene: a blind man with a cheetah on a leash, a courtesan with an ostrich-plume fan, an ephebe, a Fat Woman. And thus, when some people happen to find themselves together, taking shelter from the rain under an arcade, or crowding beneath an awning of the bazaar, or stopping to listen to the band in the square, meetings, seductions, copulations, orgies are consummated among them without a word exchanged, without a finger touching anything, almost without an eye raised.

A voluptuous vibration constantly stirs Chloe, the most chaste of cities. If men and women began to live their ephemeral dreams, every phantom would become a person with whom to begin a story of pursuits, pretenses, misunderstandings, clashes, oppressions, and the carousel of fantasies would stop.

Cities & Eyes · 1

The ancients built Valdrada on the shores of a lake, with houses all verandas one above the other, and high streets whose railed parapets look out over the water. Thus the traveler, arriving, sees two cities: one erect above the lake, and the other reflected, upside down. Nothing exists or happens in the one Valdrada that the other Valdrada does not repeat, because the city was so constructed that its every point would be reflected in its mirror, and the Valdrada down in the water contains not only all the flutings and juttings of the facades that rise above the lake, but also the rooms' interiors with ceilings and floors, the perspective of the halls, the mirrors of the wardrobes.

Valdrada's inhabitants know that each of their actions is, at once, that action and its mirror-image, which possesses the special dignity of images, and this awareness prevents them from succumbing for a single moment to chance and forgetfulness. Even when lovers twist their naked bodies, skin against skin, seeking the position that will give one the most pleasure in the other, even when murderers plunge the knife into the black veins of the neck and more clotted blood pours out the more they press the blade that slips between the tendons, it is not so much their copulating or murdering that matters as the copulating or murdering of the images, limpid and cold in the mirror.

At times the mirror increases a thing's value, at times denies it. Not everything that seems valuable above the mirror maintains its force when mirrored. The twin cities are not equal, because nothing that exists or happens in Valdrada is symmetrical: every face and gesture is answered, from the mirror, by a face and gesture inverted, point by point. The two Valdradas live for each other, their eyes interlocked; but there is no love between them.

The Great Khan has dreamed of a city; he describes it to Marco Polo:

"The harbor faces north, in shadow. The docks are high over the black water, which slams against the retaining walls; stone steps descend, made slippery by seaweed. Boats smeared with tar are tied up, waiting for the departing passengers lingering on the quay to bid their families farewell. The farewells take place in silence, but with tears. It is cold; all wear shawls over their heads. A shout from the boatman puts a stop to the delays; the traveler huddles at the prow, moves off looking toward the group of those remaining behind; from the shore his features can no longer be discerned; the boat draws up beside a vessel riding at anchor; on the ladder a diminished form climbs up, vanishes; the rusted chain is heard being raised, scraping against the hawsepipe. The people remaining behind look over the ramparts above the rocks of the pier, their eyes following the ship until it rounds the cape; for the last time they wave a white rag.

"Set out, explore every coast, and seek this city," the Khan says to Marco. "Then come back and tell me if my dream corresponds to reality."

"Forgive me, my lord, there is no doubt that sooner or later I shall set sail from that dock," Marco says, "but I *shall not come back to tell you about it. The city exists and it has a simple secret: it knows only departures, not returns."*

4

Lips clenched on the pipe's amber stem, his beard flattened against his amethyst choker, his big toes nervously arched in his silken slippers, Kublai Khan listened to Marco Polo's tales without raising an eyebrow. These were the evenings when a shadow of hypochondria weighed on his heart.

"Your cities do not exist. Perhaps they have never existed. It is sure they will never exist again. Why do you amuse yourself with consolatory fables? I know well that my empire is rotting like a corpse in a swamp, whose contagion infects the crows that peck it as well as the bamboo that grows, fertilized by its humors. Why do you not speak to me of this? Why do you lie to the emperor of the Tartars, foreigner?"

Polo knew it was best to fall in with the sovereign's dark mood. "Yes, the empire is sick, and, what is worse, it is trying to become accustomed to its sores. This is the aim of my explorations: examining the traces of happiness still to be glimpsed, I gauge its short supply. If you want to know how much darkness there is around you, you must sharpen your eyes, peering at the faint lights in the distance."

At other times, however, the Khan was seized by fits of euphoria. He would rise up on his cushions, measure with long strides the carpets spread over the paths at his feet, look out from the balustrades of the terraces to survey with dazzled eye the expanse of the palace gardens lighted by the lanterns hung from the cedars.

"And yet I know," he would say, "that my empire is made of the stuff of crystals, its molecules arranged in a perfect pattern. Amid the surge of the elements, a splendid hard diamond takes shape, an immense, faceted, transparent mountain. Why do your travel impressions stop at disappointing appearances, never catching this implacable process? Why do you linger over inessential melancholies? Why do you hide from the emperor the grandeur of his destiny?"

And Marco answered: "While, at a sign from you, sire, the unique and final city raises its stainless walls, I am collecting the ashes of the other possible cities that vanish to make room for it, cities that can never be rebuilt or remembered. When you know at last the residue of unhappiness for which no precious stone can compensate, you will be able to calculate the exact number of carats toward which that final diamond must strive. Otherwise, your calculations will be mistaken from the very start."

No one, wise Kublai, knows better than you that the city must never be confused with the words that describe it. And yet between the one and the other there is a connection. If I describe to you Olivia, a city rich in products and in profits, I can indicate its prosperity only by speaking of filigree palaces with fringed cushions on the seats by the mullioned windows. Beyond the screen of a patio, spinning jets water a lawn where a white peacock spreads its tail. But from these words you realize at once how Olivia is shrouded in a cloud of soot and grease that sticks to the houses, that in the brawling streets, the shifting trailers crush pedestrians against the walls. If I must speak to you of the inhabitants' industry, I speak of the saddlers' shops smelling of leather, of the women chattering as they weave raffia rugs, of the hanging canals whose cascades move the paddles of the mills; but the image these words evoke in your enlightened mind is of the mandrel set against the teeth of the lathe, an action repeated by thousands of hands thousands of times at the pace established for each shift. If I must explain to you how Olivia's spirit tends toward a free life and a refined civilization, I will tell you of ladies who glide at night in illuminated canoes between the banks of a green estuary; but it is only to remind you that on the outskirts where men and women land every evening like lines of sleepwalkers, there is always someone who bursts out laughing in the darkness, releasing the flow of jokes and sarcasm.

This perhaps you do not know: that to talk of Olivia, I could not use different words. If there really were an Olivia of mullioned windows and peacocks, of saddlers and rug-weavers and canoes and estuaries, it would be a wretched, black, fly-ridden hole, and to describe it, I would have to fall back on the metaphors of soot, the creaking of wheels, repeated actions, sarcasm. Falsehood is never in words; it is in things.

Thin Cities · 4

The city of Sophronia is made up of two half-cities. In one there is the great roller coaster with its steep humps, the carousel with its chain spokes, the Ferris wheel of spinning cages, the death-ride with crouching motorcyclists, the big top with the clump of trapezes hanging in the middle. The other half-city is of stone and marble and cement, with the bank, the factories, the palaces, the slaughterhouse, the school, and all the rest. One of the half-cities is permanent, the other is temporary, and when the period of its sojourn is over, they uproot it, dismantle it, and take it off, transplanting it to the vacant lots of another half-city.

And so every year the day comes when the workmen remove the marble pediments, lower the stone walls, the cement pylons, take down the Ministry, the monument, the docks, the petroleum refinery, the hospital, load them on trailers, to follow from stand to stand their annual itinerary. Here remains the half-Sophronia of the shooting-galleries and the carousels, the shout suspended from the cart of the headlong roller coaster, and it begins to count the months, the days it must wait before the caravan returns and a complete life can begin again.

Trading Cities · 3

When he enters the territory of which Eutropia is the capital, the traveler sees not one city but many, of equal size and not unlike one another, scattered over a vast, rolling plateau. Eutropia is not one, but all these cities together; only one is inhabited at a time, the others are empty; and this process is carried out in rotation. Now I shall tell you how. On the day when Eutropia's inhabitants feel the grip of weariness and no one can bear any longer his job, his relatives, his house and his life, debts, the people he must greet or who greet him, then the whole citizenry decides to move to the next city, which is there waiting for them, empty and good as new; there each will take up a new job, a different wife, will see another landscape on opening his window, and will spend his time with different pastimes, friends, gossip. So their life is renewed from move to move, among cities whose exposure or declivity or streams or winds make each site somehow different from the others. Since their society is ordered without great distinctions of wealth or authority, the passage from one function to another takes place almost without jolts; variety is guaranteed by the multiple assignments, so that in the span of a lifetime a man rarely returns to a job that has already been his.

Thus the city repeats its life, identical, shifting up and down on its empty chessboard. The inhabitants repeat the same scenes, with the actors changed; they repeat the same speeches with variously combined accents; they open alternate mouths in identical yawns. Alone, among all the cities of the empire, Eutropia remains always the same. Mercury, god of the fickle, to whom the city is sacred, worked this ambiguous miracle.

Cities & Eyes · 2

It is the mood of the beholder which gives the city of Zemrude its form. If you go by whistling, your nose a-tilt behind the whistle, you will know it from below: window sills, flapping curtains, fountains. If you walk along hanging your head, your nails dug into the palms of your hands, your gaze will be held on the ground, in the gutters, the manhole covers, the fish scales, wastepaper. You cannot say that one aspect of the city is truer than the other, but you hear of the upper Zemrude chiefly from those who remember it, as they sink into the lower Zemrude, following every day the same stretches of street and finding again each morning the ill-humor of the day before, encrusted at the foot of the walls. For everyone, sooner or later, the day comes when we bring our gaze down along the drainpipes and we can no longer detach it from the cobblestones. The reverse is not impossible, but it is more rare: and so we continue walking through Zemrude's streets with eyes now digging into the cellars, the foundations, the wells.

Cities & Names · 1

There is little I can tell you about Aglaura beyond
the things its own inhabitants have always repeated:
an array of proverbial virtues, of equally proverbial
faults, a few eccentricities, some punctilious regard
for rules. Ancient observers, whom there is no reason
not to presume truthful, attributed to Aglaura its
enduring assortment of qualities, surely comparing
them to those of the other cities of their times. Perhaps neither the Aglaura that is reported nor the
Aglaura that is visible has greatly changed since
then, but what was bizarre has become usual, what
seemed normal is now an oddity, and virtues and
faults have lost merit or dishonor in a code of virtues
and faults differently distributed. In this sense, nothing said of Aglaura is true, and yet these accounts
create a solid and compact image of a city, whereas
the haphazard opinions which might be inferred
from living there have less substance. This is the
result: the city that they speak of has much of what
is needed to exist, whereas the city that exists on its
site, exists less.

So if I wished to describe Aglaura to you, sticking
to what I personally saw and experienced, I should
have to tell you that it is a colorless city, without
character, planted there at random. But this would
not be true, either: at certain hours, in certain places
along the street, you see opening before you the hint

of something unmistakable, rare, perhaps magnificent; you would like to say what it is, but everything previously said of Aglaura imprisons your words and obliges you to repeat rather than say.

Therefore, the inhabitants still believe they live in an Aglaura which grows only with the name Aglaura and they do not notice the Aglaura that grows on the ground. And even I, who would like to keep the two cities distinct in my memory, can speak only of the one, because the recollection of the other, in the lack of words to fix it, has been lost.

"From now on, I'll describe the cities to you," the Khan had said, "in your journeys you will see if they exist."

But the cities visited by Marco Polo were always different from those thought of by the emperor.

"And yet I have constructed in my mind a model city from which all possible cities can be deduced," Kublai said. "It contains everything corresponding to the norm. Since the cities that exist diverge in varying degree from the norm, I need only foresee the exceptions to the norm and calculate the most probable combinations."

"I have also thought of a model city from which I deduce all the others," Marco answered. "It is a city made only of exceptions, exclusions, incongruities, contradictions. If such a city is the most improbable, by reducing the number of abnormal elements, we increase the probability that the city really exists. So I have only to subtract exceptions from my model, and in whatever direction I proceed, I will arrive at one of the cities which, always as an exception, exist. But I cannot force my operation beyond a certain limit: I would achieve cities too probable to be real."

5

From the high balustrade of the palace the Great Khan watches his empire grow. First the line of the boundaries had expanded to embrace conquered territories, but the regiments' advance encountered half-deserted regions, scrubby villages of huts, marshes where the rice refused to sprout, emaciated peoples, dried rivers, reeds. "My empire has grown too far toward the outside. It is time," the Khan thought, "for it to grow within itself," and he dreamed of pomegranate groves, the fruit so ripe it burst its skin, zebus browning on the spit and dripping fat, veins of metal surfacing in landslips with glistening nuggets.

Now many seasons of abundance have filled the granaries. The rivers in flood have borne forests of beams to support the bronze roofs of temples and palaces. Caravans of slaves have shifted mountains of serpentine marble across the continent. The Great Khan contemplates an empire covered with cities that weigh upon the earth and upon mankind, crammed with wealth and traffic, overladen with ornaments and offices, complicated with mechanisms and hierarchies, swollen, tense, ponderous.

"The empire is being crushed by its own weight," Kublai thinks, and in his dreams now cities light as kites appear, pierced cities like laces, cities transparent as mosquito netting, cities like leaves' veins, cities lined like a hand's palm, filigree cities to be seen through their opaque and fictitious thickness.

"I shall tell you what I dreamed last night," he says to Marco. "In the midst of a flat and yellow land, dotted with meteorites and erratic boulders, I saw from a distance the spires of a city rise, slender pinnacles, made in such a way that the moon in her journey can rest now on one, now on another, or sway from the cables of the cranes."

And Polo says: "The city of your dream is Lalage. Its inhabitants arranged these invitations to rest in the night sky so that the moon would grant everything in the city the power to grow and grow endlessly."

"There is something you do not know," the Khan adds. "The grateful moon has granted the city of Lalage a rarer privilege: to grow in lightness."

Thin Cities · 5

If you choose to believe me, good. Now I will tell how Octavia, the spider-web city, is made. There is a precipice between two steep mountains: the city is over the void, bound to the two crests with ropes and chains and catwalks. You walk on the little wooden ties, careful not to set your foot in the open spaces, or you cling to the hempen strands. Below there is nothing for hundreds and hundreds of feet: a few clouds glide past; farther down you can glimpse the chasm's bed.

This is the foundation of the city: a net which serves as passage and as support. All the rest, instead of rising up, is hung below: rope ladders, hammocks, houses made like sacks, clothes hangers, terraces like gondolas, skins of water, gas jets, spits, baskets on strings, dumb-waiters, showers, trapezes and rings for children's games, cable cars, chandeliers, pots with trailing plants.

Suspended over the abyss, the life of Octavia's inhabitants is less uncertain than in other cities. They know the net will last only so long.

Trading Cities · 4

In Ersilia, to establish the relationships that sustain the city's life, the inhabitants stretch strings from the corners of the houses, white or black or gray or black-and-white according to whether they mark a relationship of blood, of trade, authority, agency. When the strings become so numerous that you can no longer pass among them, the inhabitants leave: the houses are dismantled; only the strings and their supports remain.

From a mountainside, camping with their household goods, Ersilia's refugees look at the labyrinth of taut strings and poles that rise in the plain. That is the city of Ersilia still, and they are nothing.

They rebuild Ersilia elsewhere. They weave a similar pattern of strings which they would like to be more complex and at the same time more regular than the other. Then they abandon it and take themselves and their houses still farther away.

Thus, when traveling in the territory of Ersilia, you come upon the ruins of the abandoned cities, without the walls which do not last, without the bones of the dead which the wind rolls away: spiderwebs of intricate relationships seeking a form.

Cities & Eyes · 3

After a seven days' march through woodland, the traveler directed toward Baucis cannot see the city and yet he has arrived. The slender stilts that rise from the ground at a great distance from one another and are lost above the clouds support the city. You climb them with ladders. On the ground the inhabitants rarely show themselves: having already everything they need up there, they prefer not to come down. Nothing of the city touches the earth except those long flamingo legs on which it rests and, when the days are sunny, a pierced, angular shadow that falls on the foliage.

There are three hypotheses about the inhabitants of Baucis: that they hate the earth; that they respect it so much they avoid all contact; that they love it as it was before they existed and with spyglasses and telescopes aimed downward they never tire of examining it, leaf by leaf, stone by stone, ant by ant, contemplating with fascination their own absence.

Cities & Names · 2

Gods of two species protect the city of Leandra. Both are too tiny to be seen and too numerous to be counted. One species stands at the doors of the houses, inside, next to the coatrack and the umbrella stand; in moves, they follow the families and install themselves in the new home at the consignment of the keys. The others stay in the kitchen, hiding by preference under pots or in the chimney flue or broom closet: they belong to the house, and when the family that has lived there goes away, they remain with the new tenants; perhaps they were already there before the house existed, among the weeds of the vacant lot, concealed in a rusty can; if the house is torn down and a huge block of fifty families is built in its place, they will be found, mulitplied, in the kitchens of that many apartments. To distinguish the two species we will call the first one Penates and the other Lares.

Within a given house, Lares do not necessarily stay with Lares, and Penates with Penates: they visit one another, they stroll together on the stucco cornices, on the radiator pipes; they comment on family events; not infrequently they quarrel; but they can also get along peacefully for years—seeing them all in a row, you are unable to tell them apart. The Lares have seen Penates of the most varied origins and customs pass through their walls; the Penates have to make a place for themselves, rubbing elbows with Lares of illustrious, but decaying palaces, full of hauteur, or with Lares from tin shacks, susceptible and distrustful.

The true essence of Leandra is the subject of endless debate. The Penates believe they are the city's soul, even if they arrived last year; and they believe they take Leandra with them when they emigrate. The Lares consider the Penates temporary guests, importunate, intrusive; the real Leandra is theirs, which gives form to all it contains, the Leandra that was there before all these upstarts arrived and that will remain when all have gone away.

The two species have this in common: whatever happens in the family and in the city, they always criticize. The Penates bring out the old people, the great-grandparents, the great-aunts, the family of the past; the Lares talk about the environment before it was ruined. But this does not mean they live only on memories: they daydream of the careers the children will follow when they grow up (the Penates), or what this house in this neighborhood might become (the Lares) if it were in good hands. If you listen carefully, especially at night, you can hear them in the houses of Leandra, murmuring steadily, interrupting one another, huffing, bantering, amid ironic, stifled laughter.

Cities & the Dead · 1

At Melania, every time you enter the square, you find yourself caught in a dialogue: the braggart soldier and the parasite coming from a door meet the young wastrel and the prostitute; or else the miserly father from his threshold utters his final warnings to the amorous daughter and is interrupted by the foolish servant who is taking a note to the procuress. You return to Melania after years and you find the same dialogue still going on; in the meanwhile the parasite has died, and so have the procuress and the miserly father; but the braggart soldier, the amorous daughter, the foolish servant have taken their places, being replaced in their turn by the hypocrite, the confidante, the astrologer.

Melania's population renews itself: the participants in the dialogues die one by one and meanwhile those who will take their places are born, some in one role, some in another. When one changes role or abandons the square forever or makes his first entrance into it, there is a series of changes, until all the roles have been reassigned; but meanwhile the angry old man goes on replying to the witty maidservant, the usurer never ceases following the disinherited youth, the nurse consoles the stepdaughter, even if none of them keeps the same eyes and voice he had in the previous scene.

At times it may happen that a sole person will simultaneously take on two or more roles—tyrant, benefactor, messenger—or one role may be doubled, multiplied, assigned to a hundred, a thousand inhabitants of Melania: three thousand for the hypocrite, thirty thousand for the sponger, a hundred thousand king's sons fallen in low estate and awaiting recognition.

As time passes the roles, too, are no longer exactly the same as before; certainly the action they carry forward through intrigues and surprises leads toward some final denouement, which it continues to approach even when the plot seems to thicken more and more and the obstacles increase. If you look into the square in successive moments, you hear how from act to act the dialogue changes, even if the lives of Melania's inhabitants are too short for them to realize it.

Marco Polo describes a bridge, stone by stone.

"But which is the stone that supports the bridge?"
Kublai Khan asks.

"The bridge is not supported by one stone or another,"
Marco answers, "but by the line of the arch that they
form."

Kublai Khan remains silent, reflecting. Then he adds:
"Why do you speak to me of the stones? It is only the arch
that matters to me."

Polo answers: "Without stones there is no arch."

6

"Did you ever happen to see a city resembling this one?"
Kublai asked Marco Polo, extending his beringed hand
from beneath the silken canopy of the imperial barge, to
point to the bridges arching over the canals, the princely
palaces whose marble doorsteps were immersed in the water,
the bustle of light craft zigzagging, driven by long oars,
the boats unloading baskets of vegetables at the market
squares, the balconies, platforms, domes, campaniles, is-
land gardens glowing green in the lagoon's grayness.

The emperor, accompanied by his foreign dignitary, was
visiting Kin-sai, ancient capital of deposed dynasties, the
latest pearl set in the Great Khan's crown.

"No, sire," Marco answered, "I should never have
imagined a city like this could exist."

The emperor tried to peer into his eyes. The foreigner
lowered his gaze. Kublai remained silent the whole day.

After sunset, on the terraces of the palace, Marco Polo
expounded to the sovereign the results of his missions. As a
rule the Great Khan concluded his day savoring these tales
with half-closed eyes until his first yawn was the signal for
the suite of pages to light the flames that guided the mon-
arch to the Pavilion of the August Slumber. But this time
Kublai seemed unwilling to give in to weariness. "Tell me
another city," he insisted.

". . . You leave there and ride for three days between
the northeast and east-by-northeast winds . . . " Marco

resumed saying, enumerating names and customs and wares of a great number of lands. His repertory could be called inexhaustible, but now he was the one who had to give in. Dawn had broken when he said: "Sire, now I have told you about all the cities I know."

"There is still one of which you never speak."

Marco Polo bowed his head.

"Venice," the Khan said.

Marco smiled. "What else do you believe I have been talking to you about?"

The emperor did not turn a hair. "And yet I have never heard you mention that name."

And Polo said: "Every time I describe a city I am saying something about Venice."

"When I ask you about other cities, I want to hear about them. And about Venice, when I ask you about Venice."

"To distinguish the other cities' qualities, I must speak of a first city that remains implicit. For me it is Venice."

"You should then begin each tale of your travels from the departure, describing Venice as it is, all of it, not omitting anything you remember of it."

The lake's surface was barely wrinkled; the copper reflection of the ancient palace of the Sung was shattered into sparkling glints like floating leaves.

"Memory's images, once they are fixed in words, are erased," Polo said. "Perhaps I am afraid of losing Venice all at once, if I speak of it. Or perhaps, speaking of other cities, I have already lost it, little by little."

Trading Cities · 5

In Esmeralda, city of water, a network of canals and a network of streets span and intersect each other. To go from one place to another you have always the choice between land and boat: and since the shortest distance between two points in Esmeralda is not a straight line but a zigzag that ramifies in tortuous optional routes, the ways that open to each passerby are never two, but many, and they increase further for those who alternate a stretch by boat with one on dry land.

And so Esmeralda's inhabitants are spared the boredom of following the same streets every day. And that is not all: the network of routes is not arranged on one level, but follows instead an up-and-down course of steps, landings, cambered bridges, hanging streets. Combining segments of the various routes, elevated or on ground level, each inhabitant can enjoy every day the pleasure of a new itinerary to reach the same places. The most fixed and calm lives in Esmeralda are spent without any repetition.

Secret and adventurous lives, here as elsewhere, are subject to greater restrictions. Esmeralda's cats, thieves, illicit lovers move along higher, discontinuous ways, dropping from a rooftop to a balcony, following gutterings with acrobats' steps. Below, the rats run in the darkness of the sewers, one behind the other's tail, along with conspirators and smugglers:

they peep out of manholes and drainpipes, they slip through double bottoms and ditches, from one hiding place to another they drag crusts of cheese, contraband goods, kegs of gunpowder, crossing the city's compactness pierced by the spokes of underground passages.

A map of Esmeralda should include, marked in different colored inks, all these routes, solid and liquid, evident and hidden. It is more difficult to fix on the map the routes of the swallows, who cut the air over the roofs, dropping long invisible parabolas with their still wings, darting to gulp a mosquito, spiraling upward, grazing a pinnacle, dominating from every point of their airy paths all the points of the city.

Cities & Eyes · 4

When you have arrived at Phyllis, you rejoice in observing all the bridges over the canals, each different from the others: cambered, covered, on pillars, on barges, suspended, with tracery balustrades. And what a variety of windows looks down on the streets: mullioned, Moorish, lancet, pointed, surmounted by lunettes or stained-glass roses; how many kinds of pavement cover the ground: cobbles, slabs, gravel, blue and white tiles. At every point the city offers surprises to your view: a caper bush jutting from the fortress' walls, the statues of three queens on corbels, an onion dome with three smaller onions threaded on the spire. "Happy the man who has Phyllis before his eyes each day and who never ceases seeing the things it contains," you cry, with regret at having to leave the city when you can barely graze it with your glance.

But it so happens that, instead, you must stay in Phyllis and spend the rest of your days there. Soon the city fades before your eyes, the rose windows are expunged, the statues on the corbels, the domes. Like all of Phyllis's inhabitants, you follow zigzag lines from one street to another, you distinguish the patches of sunlight from the patches of shade, a door here, a stairway there, a bench where you can put down your basket, a hole where your foot stumbles if you are not careful. All the rest of the city is invisible. Phyllis is a space in which routes are drawn between points suspended in the void: the shortest way to reach that certain merchant's tent, avoiding that certain creditor's window. Your footsteps follow not what is outside the eyes, but what is within, buried, erased. If, of two arcades, one continues to seem more joyous, it is because thirty years ago a girl went by there, with broad, embroidered sleeves, or else it is only because that arcade catches the light at a certain hour like that other arcade, you cannot recall where.

Millions of eyes look up at windows, bridges, capers, and they might be scanning a blank page. Many are the cities like Phyllis, which elude the gaze of all, except the man who catches them by surprise.

Cities & Names · 3

For a long time Pyrrha to me was a fortified city on the slopes of a bay, with high windows and towers, enclosed like a goblet, with a central square deep as a well, with a well in its center. I had never seen it. It was one of the many cities where I had never arrived, that I conjured up, through its name: Euphrasia, Odile, Margara, Getullia. Pyrrha had its place among them, different from each of them, and like each of them, unmistakable to the mind's eye.

The day came when my travels took me to Pyrrha. As soon as I set foot there, everything I had imagined was forgotten; Pyrrha had become what is Pyrrha; and I thought I had always known that the sea is invisible from the city, hidden behind a dune of the low, rolling coast; that the streets are long and straight; that the houses are clumped at intervals, not high, and they are separated by open lots with stacks of lumber and with sawmills; that the wind stirs the vanes of the water pumps. From that moment on the name Pyrrha has brought to my mind this view, this light, this buzzing, this air in which a yellowish dust flies: obviously the name means this and could mean nothing but this.

My mind goes on containing a great number of cities I have never seen and will never see, names that bear with them a figure or a fragment or glimmer of an imagined figure: Getullia, Odile, Euphrasia, Margara. The city high above the bay is also there still, with the square enclosing the well, but I can no longer call it by a name, nor remember how I could ever have given it a name that means something entirely different.

Cities & the Dead · 2

Never in all my travels had I ventured as far as Adelma. It was dusk when I landed there. On the dock the sailor who caught the rope and tied it to the bollard resembled a man who had soldiered with me and was dead. It was the hour of the wholesale fish market. An old man was loading a basket of sea urchins on a cart; I thought I recognized him; when I turned, he had disappeared down an alley, but I realized that he looked like a fisherman who, already old when I was a child, could no longer be among the living. I was upset by the sight of a fever victim huddled on the ground, a blanket over his head: my father a few days before his death had yellow eyes and a growth of beard like this man. I turned my gaze aside; I no longer dared look anyone in the face.

I thought: "If Adelma is a city I am seeing in a dream, where you encounter only the dead, the dream frightens me. If Adelma is a real city, inhabited by living people, I need only continue looking at them and the resemblances will dissolve, alien faces will appear, bearing anguish. In either case it is best for me not to insist on staring at them."

A vegetable vendor was weighing a cabbage on a scales and put it in a basket dangling on a string a girl lowered from a balcony. The girl was identical with one in my village who had gone mad for love and killed herself. The vegetable vendor raised her face: she was my grandmother.

I thought: "You reach a moment in life when, among the people you have known, the dead outnumber the living. And the mind refuses to accept more faces, more expressions: on every new face you encounter, it prints the old forms, for each one it finds the most suitable mask."

The stevedores climbed the steps in a line, bent beneath demijohns and barrels; their faces were hidden by sackcloth hoods; "Now they will straighten up and I will recognize them," I thought, with impatience and fear. But I could not take my eyes off them; if I turned my gaze just a little toward the crowd that crammed those narrow streets, I was assailed by unexpected faces, reappearing from far away, staring at me as if demanding recognition, as if to recognize me, as if they had already recognized me. Perhaps, for each of them, I also resembled someone who was dead. I had barely arrived at Adelma and I was already one of them, I had gone over to their side, absorbed in that kaleidoscope of eyes, wrinkles, grimaces.

I thought: "Perhaps Adelma is the city where you arrive dying and where each finds again the people he has known. This means I, too, am dead." And I also thought: "This means the beyond is not happy."

Cities & the Sky · 1

In Eudoxia, which spreads both upward and down, with winding alleys, steps, dead ends, hovels, a carpet is preserved in which you can observe the city's true form. At first sight nothing seems to resemble Eudoxia less than the design of that carpet, laid out in symmetrical motives whose patterns are repeated along straight and circular lines, interwoven with brilliantly colored spires, in a repetition that can be followed throughout the whole woof. But if you pause and examine it carefully, you become convinced that each place in the carpet corresponds to a place in the city and all the things contained in the city are included in the design, arranged according to their true relationship, which escapes your eye distracted by the bustle, the throngs, the shoving. All of Eudoxia's confusion, the mules' braying, the lampblack stains, the fish smell is what is evident in the incomplete perspective you grasp; but the carpet proves that there is a point from which the city shows its true proportions, the geometrical scheme implicit in its every, tiniest detail.

It is easy to get lost in Eudoxia: but when you concentrate and stare at the carpet, you recognize the street you were seeking in a crimson or indigo or magenta thread which, in a wide loop, brings you to the purple enclosure that is your real destination. Every inhabitant of Eudoxia compares the carpet's immobile order with his own image of the city, an anguish of his own, and each can find, concealed among the arabesques, an answer, the story of his life, the twists of fate.

An oracle was questioned about the mysterious bond between two objects so dissimilar as the carpet and the city. One of the two objects—the oracle replied—has the form the gods gave the starry sky and the orbits in which the worlds revolve; the other is an approximate reflection, like every human creation.

For some time the augurs had been sure that the carpet's harmonious pattern was of divine origin. The oracle was interpreted in this sense, arousing no controversy. But you could, similarly, come to the opposite conclusion: that the true map of the universe is the city of Eudoxia, just as it is, a stain that spreads out shapelessly, with crooked streets, houses that crumble one upon the other amid clouds of dust, fires, screams in the darkness.

". . . So then, yours is truly a journey through memory!" The Great Khan, his ears always sharp, sat up in his hammock every time he caught the hint of a sigh in Marco's speech. "It was to slough off a burden of nostalgia that you went so far away!" he exclaimed, or else: "You return from your voyages with a cargo of regrets!" And he added, sarcastically: "Meager purchases, to tell the truth, for a merchant of the Serenissima!"

This was the target of all Kublai's questions about the past and the future. For an hour he had been toying with it, like a cat with a mouse, and finally he had Marco with his back to the wall, attacking him, putting a knee on his chest, seizing him by the beard: "This is what I wanted to hear from you: confess what you are smuggling: moods, states of grace, elegies!"

These words and actions were perhaps only imagined, as the two, silent and motionless, watched the smoke rise slowly from their pipes. The cloud dissolved at times in a wisp of wind, or else remained suspended in mid-air; and the answer was in that cloud. As the puff carried the smoke away, Marco thought of the mists that cloud the expanse of the sea and the mountain ranges and, when dispelled, leave the air dry and diaphanous, revealing distant cities. It was beyond that screen of fickle humors that his gaze wished to arrive: the form of things can be discerned better at a distance.

Or else the cloud hovered, having barely left the lips,

dense and slow, and suggested another vision: the exhalations that hang over the roofs of the metropolises, the opaque smoke that is not scattered, the hood of miasmata that weighs over the bituminous streets. Not the labile mists of memory nor the dry transparence, but the charring of burned lives that forms a scab on the city, the sponge swollen with vital matter that no longer flows, the jam of past, present, future that blocks existences calcified in the illusion of movement: this is what you would find at the end of your journey.

7

KUBLAI: *I do not know when you have had time to visit all the countries you describe to me. It seems to me you have never moved from this garden.*

POLO: *Everything I see and do assumes meaning in a mental space where the same calm reigns as here, the same penumbra, the same silence streaked by the rustling of leaves. At the moment when I concentrate and reflect, I find myself again, always, in this garden, at this hour of the evening, in your august presence, though I continue, without a moment's pause, moving up a river green with crocodiles or counting the barrels of salted fish being lowered into the hold.*

KUBLAI: *I, too, am not sure I am here, strolling among the porphyry fountains, listening to the plashing echo, and not riding, caked with sweat and blood, at the head of my army, conquering the lands you will have to describe, or cutting off the fingers of the attackers scaling the walls of a besieged fortress.*

POLO: *Perhaps this garden exists only in the shadow of our lowered eyelids, and we have never stopped: you, from raising dust on the fields of battle; and I, from bargaining for sacks of pepper in distant bazaars. But each time we half-close our eyes, in the midst of the din and the throng, we are allowed to withdraw here, dressed in silk kimonos, to ponder what we are seeing and living, to draw conclusions, to contemplate from the distance.*

KUBLAI: *Perhaps this dialogue of ours is taking place between two beggars nicknamed Kublai Khan and Marco Polo; as they sift through a rubbish heap, piling up rusted flotsam, scraps of cloth, wastepaper, while drunk on the few sips of bad wine, they see all the treasure of the East shine around them.*

POLO: *Perhaps all that is left of the world is a wasteland covered with rubbish heaps, and the hanging garden of the Great Khan's palace. It is our eyelids that separate them, but we cannot know which is inside and which outside.*

Cities & Eyes · 5

When you have forded the river, when you have crossed the mountain pass, you suddenly find before you the city of Moriana, its alabaster gates transparent in the sunlight, its coral columns supporting pediments encrusted with serpentine, its villas all of glass like aquariums where the shadows of dancing girls with silvery scales swim beneath the medusa-shaped chandeliers. If this is not your first journey, you already know that cities like this have an obverse: you have only to walk in a semicircle and you will come into view of Moriana's hidden face, an expanse of rusting sheet metal, sackcloth, planks bristling with spikes, pipes black with soot, piles of tins, blind walls with fading signs, frames of staved-in straw chairs, ropes good only for hanging oneself from a rotten beam.

From one part to the other, the city seems to continue, in perspective, multiplying its repertory of images: but instead it has no thickness, it consists only of a face and an obverse, like a sheet of paper, with a figure on either side, which can neither be separated nor look at each other.

Cities & Names · 4

Clarice, the glorious city, has a tormented history. Several times it decayed, then burgeoned again, always keeping the first Clarice as an unparalleled model of every splendor, compared to which the city's present state can only cause more sighs at every fading of the stars.

In its centuries of decadence, emptied by plagues, its height reduced by collapsing beams and cornices and by shifts of the terrain, rusted and stopped up through neglect or the lack of maintenance men, the city slowly became populated again as the survivors emerged from the basements and lairs, in hordes, swarming like rats, driven by their fury to rummage and gnaw, and yet also to collect and patch, like nesting birds. They grabbed everything that could be taken from where it was and put it in another place to serve a different use: brocade curtains ended up as sheets; in marble funerary urns they planted basil; wrought-iron gratings torn from the harem windows were used for roasting cat-meat on fires of inlaid wood. Put together with odd bits of the useless Clarice, a survivors' Clarice was taking shape, all huts and hovels, festering sewers, rabbit cages. And yet, almost nothing was lost of Clarice's former splendor; it was all there, merely arranged in a different order, no less appropriate to the inhabitants' needs than it had been before.

The days of poverty were followed by more joyous times: a sumptuous butterfly-Clarice emerged from the beggared chrysalis-Clarice. The new abundance made the city overflow with new materials, buildings, objects; new people flocked in from outside; nothing, no one had any connection with the former Clarice, or Clarices. And the more the new city settled triumphantly into the place and the name of the first Clarice, the more it realized it was moving away from it, destroying it no less rapidly than the rats and the mold. Despite its pride in its new wealth, the city, at heart, felt itself incongruous, alien, a usurper.

And then the shards of the original splendor that had been saved, by adapting them to more obscure needs, were again shifted. They were now preserved under glass bells, locked in display cases, set on velvet cushions, and not because they might still be used for anything, but because people wanted to reconstruct through them a city of which no one knew anything now.

More decadences, more burgeonings have followed one another in Clarice. Populations and customs have changed several times; the name, the site, and the objects hardest to break remain. Each new Clarice, compact as a living body with its smells and its breath, shows off, like a gem, what remains of the ancient Clarices, fragmentary and dead. There is no knowing when the Corinthian capitals stood on the top of their columns: only one of them is remembered, since for many years, in a chicken run, it supported the basket where the hens laid their eggs, and from there it was moved to the Museum of Capitals, in line with other specimens of the collection. The order of the eras' succession has been lost; that a first Clarice existed is a widespread belief, but there are no proofs to support it. The capitals could have been in the chicken runs before they were in the temples, the marble urns could have been planted with basil before they were filled with dead bones. Only this is known for sure: a given number of objects is shifted within a given space, at times submerged by a quantity of new objects, at times worn out and not replaced; the rule is to shuffle them each time, then try to assemble them. Perhaps Clarice has always been only a confusion of chipped gimcracks, ill-assorted, obsolete.

Cities & the Dead · 3

No city is more inclined than Eusapia to enjoy life and flee care. And to make the leap from life to death less abrupt, the inhabitants have constructed an identical copy of their city, underground. All corpses, dried in such a way that the skeleton remains sheathed in yellow skin, are carried down there, to continue their former activities. And, of these activities, it is their carefree moments that take first place: most of the corpses are seated around laden tables, or placed in dancing positions, or made to play little trumpets. But all the trades and professions of the living Eusapia are also at work below ground, or at least those that the living performed with more contentment than irritation: the clockmaker, amid all the stopped clocks of his shop, places his parchment ear against an out-of-tune grandfather's clock; a barber, with dry brush, lathers the cheekbones of an actor learning his role, studying the script with hollow sockets; a girl with a laughing skull milks the carcass of a heifer.

To be sure, many of the living want a fate after death different from their lot in life: the necropolis is crowded with big-game hunters, mezzosopranos, bankers, violinists, duchesses, courtesans, generals—more than the living city ever contained.

The job of accompanying the dead down below and arranging them in the desired place is assigned to a confraternity of hooded brothers. No one else has access to the Eusapia of the dead and everything known about it has been learned from them.

They say that the same confraternity exists among the dead and that it never fails to lend a hand; the hooded brothers, after death, will perform the same job in the other Eusapia; rumor has it that some of them are already dead but continue going up and down. In any case, this confraternity's authority in the Eusapia of the living is vast.

They say that every time they go below they find something changed in the lower Eusapia; the dead make innovations in their city; not many, but surely the fruit of sober reflection, not passing whims. From one year to the next, they say, the Eusapia of the dead becomes unrecognizable. And the living, to keep up with them, also want to do everything that the hooded brothers tell them about the novelties of the dead. So the Eusapia of the living has taken to copying its underground copy.

They say that this has not just now begun to happen: actually it was the dead who built the upper Eusapia, in the image of their city. They say that in the twin cities there is no longer any way of knowing who is alive and who is dead.

Cities & the Sky · 2

This belief is handed down in Beersheba: that, suspended in the heavens, there exists another Beersheba, where the city's most elevated virtues and sentiments are poised, and that if the terrestrial Beersheba will take the celestial one as its model the two cities will become one. The image propagated by tradition is that of a city of pure gold, with silver locks and diamond gates, a jewel-city, all inset and inlaid, as a maximum of laborious study might produce when applied to materials of the maximum worth. True to this belief, Beersheba's inhabitants honor everything that suggests for them the celestial city: they accumulate noble metals and rare stones, they renounce all ephemeral excesses, they develop forms of composite composure.

They also believe, these inhabitants, that another Beersheba exists underground, the receptacle of everything base and unworthy that happens to them, and it is their constant care to erase from the visible Beersheba every tie or resemblance to the lower twin. In the place of roofs they imagine that the underground city has overturned rubbish bins, with cheese rinds, greasy paper, fish scales, dishwater, uneaten spaghetti, old bandages spilling from them. Or even that its substance is dark and malleable and thick, like the pitch that pours down from the sewers, prolonging the route of the human bowels, from black hole to black hole, until it splatters against the lowest subterranean floor, and from the lazy, encircled bubbles below, layer upon layer, a fecal city rises, with twisted spires.

In Beersheba's beliefs there is an element of truth and one of error. It is true that the city is accompanied by two projections of itself, one celestial and one infernal; but the citizens are mistaken about their consistency. The inferno that broods in the deepest subsoil of Beersheba is a city designed by the most authoritative architects, built with the most expensive materials on the market, with every device and mechanism and gear system functioning, decked with tassels and fringes and frills hanging from all the pipes and levers.

Intent on piling up its carats of perfection, Beersheba takes for virtue what is now a grim mania to fill the empty vessel of itself; the city does not know that its only moments of generous abandon are those when it becomes detached from itself, when it lets go, expands. Still, at the zenith of Beersheba there gravitates a celestial body that shines with all the city's riches, enclosed in the treasury of cast-off things: a planet a-flutter with potato peels, broken umbrellas, old socks, candy wrappings, paved with tram tickets, fingernail-cuttings and pared calluses, eggshells. This is the celestial city, and in its heavens long-tailed comets fly past, released to rotate in space from the only free and happy action of the citizens of Beersheba, a city which, only when it shits, is not miserly, calculating, greedy.

The city of Leonia refashions itself every day: every morning the people wake between fresh sheets, wash with just-unwrapped cakes of soap, wear brand-new clothing, take from the latest model refrigerator still unopened tins, listening to the last-minute jingles from the most up-to-date radio.

On the sidewalks, encased in spotless plastic bags, the remains of yesterday's Leonia await the garbage truck. Not only squeezed tubes of toothpaste, blown-out light bulbs, newspapers, containers, wrappings, but also boilers, encyclopedias, pianos, procelain dinner services. It is not so much by the things that each day are manufactured, sold, bought that you can measure Leonia's opulence, but rather by the things that each day are thrown out to make room for the new. So you begin to wonder if Leonia's true passion is really, as they say, the enjoyment of new and different things, and not, instead, the joy of expelling, discarding, cleansing itself of a recurrent impurity. The fact is that street cleaners are welcomed like angels, and their task of removing the residue of yesterday's existence is surrounded by a respectful silence, like a ritual that inspires devotion, perhaps only because once things have been cast off nobody wants to have to think about them further.

Nobody wonders where, each day, they carry their load of refuse. Outside the city, surely; but each year the city expands, and the street cleaners have to fall farther back. The bulk of the outflow increases and the piles rise higher, become stratified, extend over a wider perimeter. Besides, the more Leonia's talent for making new materials excels, the more the rubbish improves in quality, resists time, the elements, fermentations, combustions. A fortress of indestructible leftovers surrounds Leonia, dominating it on every side, like a chain of mountains.

This is the result: the more Leonia expels goods, the more it accumulates them; the scales of its past are soldered into a cuirass that cannot be removed. As the city is renewed each day, it preserves all of itself in its only definitive form: yesterday's sweepings piled up on the sweepings of the day before yesterday and of all its days and years and decades.

Leonia's rubbish little by little would invade the world, if, from beyond the final crest of its boundless rubbish heap, the street cleaners of other cities were not pressing, also pushing mountains of refuse in front of themselves. Perhaps the whole world, beyond Leonia's boundaries, is covered by craters of rubbish, each surrounding a metropolis in constant eruption. The boundaries between the alien, hostile cities are infected ramparts where the detritus of both support each other, overlap, mingle.

The greater its height grows, the more the danger

of a landslide looms: a tin can, an old tire, an unraveled wine flask, if it rolls toward Leonia, is enough to bring with it an avalanche of unmated shoes, calendars of bygone years, withered flowers, submerging the city in its own past, which it had tried in vain to reject, mingling with the past of the neighboring cities, finally clean. A cataclysm will flatten the sordid mountain range, canceling every trace of the metropolis always dressed in new clothes. In the nearby cities they are all ready, waiting with bulldozers to flatten the terrain, to push into the new territory, expand, and drive the new street cleaners still farther out.

POLO: . . . Perhaps the terraces of this garden overlook only the lake of our mind. . . .

KUBLAI: . . . and however far our troubled enterprises as warriors and merchants may take us, we both harbor within ourselves this silent shade, this conversation of pauses, this evening that is always the same.

POLO: Unless the opposite hypothesis is correct: that those who strive in camps and ports exist only because we two think of them, here, enclosed among these bamboo hedges, motionless since time began.

KUBLAI: Unless toil, shouts, sores, stink do not exist; and only this azalea bush.

POLO: Unless porters, stonecutters, rubbish collectors, cooks cleaning the lights of chickens, washerwomen bent over stones, mothers stirring rice as they nurse their infants, exist only because we think them.

KUBLAI: To tell the truth, I never think them.

POLO: Then they do not exist.

KUBLAI: To me this conjecture does not seem to suit our purposes. Without them we could never remain here swaying, cocooned in our hammocks.

POLO: *Then the hypothesis must be rejected. So the other hypothesis is true: they exist and we do not.*

KUBLAI: *We have proved that if we were here, we would not be.*

POLO: *And here, in fact, we are.*

8

From the foot of the Great Khan's throne a majolica pavement extended. Marco Polo, mute informant, spread out on it the samples of the wares he had brought back from his journeys to the ends of the empire: a helmet, a seashell, a coconut, a fan. Arranging the objects in a certain order on the black and white tiles, and occasionally shifting them with studied moves, the ambassador tried to depict for the monarch's eyes the vicissitudes of his travels, the conditions of the empire, the prerogatives of the distant provincial seats.

Kublai was a keen chess player; following Marco's movements, he observed that certain pieces implied or excluded the vicinity of other pieces and were shifted along certain lines. Ignoring the objects' variety of form, he could grasp the system of arranging one with respect to the others on the majolica floor. He thought: "If each city is like a game of chess, the day when I have learned the rules, I shall finally possess my empire, even if I shall never succeed in knowing all the cities it contains."

Actually, it was useless for Marco's speeches to employ all this bric-a-brac: a chessboard would have sufficed, with its specific pieces. To each piece, in turn, they could give an appropriate meaning: a knight could stand for a real horseman, or for a procession of coaches, an army on the march, an equestrian monument: a queen could be a lady looking down from her balcony, a fountain, a church with a pointed dome, a quince tree.

Returning from his last mission, Marco Polo found the Khan awaiting him, seated at a chessboard. With a gesture he invited the Venetian to sit opposite him and describe, with the help only of the chessmen, the cities he had visited. Marco did not lose heart. The Great Khan's chessmen were huge pieces of polished ivory: arranging on the board looming rooks and sulky knights, assembling swarms of pawns, drawing straight or oblique avenues like a queen's progress, Marco recreated the perspectives and the spaces of black and white cities on moonlit nights.

Contemplating these essential landscapes, Kublai reflected on the invisible order that sustains cities, on the rules that decreed how they rise, take shape and prosper, adapting themselves to the seasons, and then how they sadden and fall in ruins. At times he thought he was on the verge of discovering a coherent, harmonious system underlying the infinite deformities and discords, but no model could stand up to the comparison with the game of chess. Perhaps, instead of racking one's brain to suggest with the ivory pieces' scant help visions which were anyway destined to oblivion, it would suffice to play a game according to the rules, and to consider each successive state of the board as one of the countless forms that the system of forms assembles and destroys.

Now Kublai Khan no longer had to send Marco Polo on distant expeditions: he kept him playing endless games of chess. Knowledge of the empire was hidden in the pattern drawn by the angular shifts of the knight, by the diagonal passages opened by the bishop's incursions, by the lumbering, cautious tread of the king and the humble pawn, by the inexorable ups and downs of every game.

The Great Khan tried to concentrate on the game: but now it was the game's purpose that eluded him. Each game ends in a gain or a loss: but of what? What were the true stakes? At checkmate, beneath the foot of the king, knocked aside by the winner's hand, a black or a white square remains. By disembodying his conquests to reduce them to the essential, Kublai had arrived at the extreme operation: the definitive conquest, of which the empire's multiform treasures were only illusory envelopes. It was reduced to a square of planed wood: nothingness. . . .

Cities & Names · 5

Irene is the city visible when you lean out from the edge of the plateau at the hour when the lights come on, and in the limpid air, the pink of the settlement can be discerned spread out in the distance below: where the windows are more concentrated, where it thins out in dimly lighted alleys, where it collects the shadows of gardens, where it raises towers with signal fires; and if the evening is misty, a hazy glow swells like a milky sponge at the foot of the gulleys.

Travelers on the plateau, shepherds shifting their flocks, bird-catchers watching their nets, hermits gathering greens: all look down and speak of Irene. At times the wind brings a music of bass drums and trumpets, the bang of firecrackers in the light-display of a festival; at times the rattle of guns, the explosion of a powder magazine in the sky yellow with the fires of civil war. Those who look down from the heights conjecture about what is happening in the city; they wonder if it would be pleasant or unpleasant to be in Irene that evening. Not that they have any intention of going there (in any case the roads winding down to the valley are bad), but Irene is a magnet for the eyes and thoughts of those who stay up above.

At this point Kublai Khan expects Marco to speak of Irene as it is seen from within. But Marco cannot do this: he has not succeeded in discovering which is the city that those of the plateau call Irene. For that matter, it is of slight importance: if you saw it, standing in its midst, it would be a different city; Irene is a name for a city in the distance, and if you approach, it changes.

For those who pass it without entering, the city is one thing; it is another for those who are trapped by it and never leave. There is the city where you arrive for the first time; and there is another city which you leave never to return. Each deserves a different name; perhaps I have already spoken of Irene under other names; perhaps I have spoken only of Irene.

Cities & the Dead · 4

What makes Argia different from other cities is that it has earth instead of air. The streets are completely filled with dirt, clay packs the rooms to the ceiling, on every stair another stairway is set in negative, over the roofs of the houses hang layers of rocky terrain like skies with clouds. We do not know if the inhabitants can move about the city, widening the worm tunnels and the crevices where roots twist: the dampness destroys people's bodies and they have scant strength; everyone is better off remaining still, prone; anyway, it is dark.

From up here, nothing of Argia can be seen; some say, "It's down below there," and we can only believe them. The place is deserted. At night, putting your ear to the ground, you can sometimes hear a door slam.

Cities & the Sky · 3

Those who arrive at Thekla can see little of the city, beyond the plank fences, the sackcloth screens, the scaffoldings, the metal armatures, the wooden cat-walks hanging from ropes or supported by sawhorses, the ladders, the trestles. If you ask, "Why is Thekla's construction taking such a long time?" the inhabitants continue hoisting sacks, lowering leaded strings, moving long brushes up and down, as they answer, "So that its destruction cannot begin." And if asked whether they fear that, once the scaffoldings are removed, the city may begin to crumble and fall to pieces, they add hastily, in a whisper, "Not only the city."

If, dissatisfied with the answers, someone puts his eye to a crack in a fence, he sees cranes pulling up other cranes, scaffoldings that embrace other scaf-foldings, beams that prop up other beams. "What meaning does your construction have?" he asks. "What is the aim of a city under construction unless it is a city? Where is the plan you are following, the blueprint?"

"We will show it to you as soon as the working day is over; we cannot interrupt our work now," they answer.

Work stops at sunset. Darkness falls over the building site. The sky is filled with stars. "There is the blueprint," they say.

Continuous Cities · 2

If on arriving at Trude I had not read the city's name written in big letters, I would have thought I was landing at the same airport from which I had taken off. The suburbs they drove me through were no different from the others, with the same little greenish and yellowish houses. Following the same signs we swung around the same flower beds in the same squares. The downtown streets displayed goods, packages, signs that had not changed at all. This was the first time I had come to Trude, but I already knew the hotel where I happened to be lodged; I had already heard and spoken my dialogues with the buyers and sellers of hardware; I had ended other days identically, looking through the same goblets at the same swaying navels.

Why come to Trude? I asked myself. And I already wanted to leave.

"You can resume your flight whenever you like," they said to me, "but you will arrive at another Trude, absolutely the same, detail by detail. The world is covered by a sole Trude which does not begin and does not end. Only the name of the airport changes."

Hidden Cities · 1

In Olinda, if you go out with a magnifying glass and hunt carefully, you may find somewhere a point no bigger than the head of a pin which, if you look at it slightly enlarged, reveals within itself the roofs, the antennas, the skylights, the gardens, the pools, the streamers across the streets, the kiosks in the squares, the horse-racing track. That point does not remain there: a year later you will find it the size of half a lemon, then as large as a mushroom, then a soup plate. And then it becomes a full-size city, enclosed within the earlier city: a new city that forces its way ahead in the earlier city and presses it toward the outside.

Olinda is certainly not the only city that grows in concentric circles, like tree trunks which each year add one more ring. But in other cities there remains, in the center, the old narrow girdle of the walls from which the withered spires rise, the towers, the tiled roofs, the domes, while the new quarters sprawl around them like a loosened belt. Not Olinda: the old walls expand bearing the old quarters with them, enlarged, but maintaining their proportions on a broader horizon at the edges of the city; they surround the slightly newer quarters, which also grew up on the margins and became thinner to make room for still more recent ones pressing from inside; and so, on and on, to the heart of the city, a totally new

Olinda which, in its reduced dimensions retains the features and the flow of lymph of the first Olinda and of all the Olindas that have blossomed one from the other; and within this innermost circle there are already blossoming—though it is hard to discern them—the next Olinda and those that will grow after it. ·

. . . The Great Khan tried to concentrate on the game: but now it was the game's reason that eluded him. The end of every game is a gain or a loss: but of what? What were the real stakes? At checkmate, beneath the foot of the king, knocked aside by the winner's hand, nothingness remains: a black square, or a white one. By disembodying his conquests to reduce them to the essential, Kublai had arrived at the extreme operation: the definitive conquest, of which the empire's multiform treasures were only illusory envelopes; it was reduced to a square of planed wood.

Then Marco Polo spoke: "Your chessboard, sire, is inlaid with two woods: ebony and maple. The square on which your enlightened gaze is fixed was cut from the ring of a trunk that grew in a year of drought: you see how its fibers are arranged? Here a barely hinted knot can be made out: a bud tried to burgeon on a premature spring day, but the night's frost forced it to desist."

Until then the Great Khan had not realized that the foreigner knew how to express himself fluently in his language, but it was not this fluency that amazed him.

"Here is a thicker pore: perhaps it was a larvum's nest; not a woodworm, because, once born, it would have begun to dig, but a caterpillar that gnawed the leaves and was the cause of the tree's being chosen for chopping down . . . This edge was scored by the wood carver with his gouge so that it would adhere to the next square, more protruding. . . ."

The quantity of things that could be read in a little piece of smooth and empty wood overwhelmed Kublai; Polo was already talking about ebony forests, about rafts laden with logs that come down the rivers, of docks, of women at the windows. . . .

9

The Great Khan owns an atlas where all the cities of the empire and the neighboring realms are drawn, building by building and street by street, with walls, rivers, bridges, harbors, cliffs. He realizes that from Marco Polo's tales it is pointless to expect news of those places, which for that matter he knows well: how at Kambalu, capital of China, three square cities stand one within the other, each with four temples and four gates that are opened according to the seasons; how on the island of Java the rhinoceros rages, charging, with his murderous horn; how pearls are gathered on the ocean bed off the coasts of Malabar.

Kublai asks Marco, "When you return to the West, will you repeat to your people the same tales you tell me?"

"I speak and speak," Marco says, "but the listener retains only the words he is expecting. The description of the world to which you lend a benevolent ear is one thing; the description that will go the rounds of the groups of stevedores and gondoliers on the street outside my house the day of my return is another; and yet another, that which I might dictate late in life, if I were taken prisoner by Genoese pirates and put in irons in the same cell with a writer of adventure stories. It is not the voice that commands the story: it is the ear."

"At times I feel your voice is reaching me from far away, while I am prisoner of a gaudy and unlivable present, where all forms of human society have reached an extreme of their cycle and there is no imagining what new forms they may assume. And I hear, from your voice, the invisible reasons which make cities live, through which perhaps, once dead, they will come to life again."

The Great Khan owns an atlas whose drawings depict the terrestrial globe all at once and continent by continent, the borders of the most distant realms, the ships' routes, the coastlines, the maps of the most illustrious metropolises and of the most opulent ports. He leafs through the maps before Marco Polo's eyes to put his knowledge to the test. The traveler recognizes Constantinople in the city which from three shores dominates a long strait, a narrow gulf, and an enclosed sea; he remembers that Jerusalem is set on two hills, of unequal height, facing each other; he has no hesitation in pointing to Samarkand and its gardens.

For other cities he falls back on descriptions handed down by word of mouth, or he guesses on the basis of scant indications: and so Granada, the streaked pearl of the caliphs; Lübeck, the neat, boreal port; Timbuktu, black with ebony and white with ivory; Paris, where millions of men come home every day grasping a wand of bread. In colored miniatures the atlas depicts inhabited places of unusual form: an oasis hidden in a fold of the desert from which only palm crests peer out is surely Nefta; a castle amid quicksands and cows grazing in meadows salted by the tides can only suggest Mont-Saint-Michel; and a palace that instead of rising within a city's walls contains within its own walls a city can only be Urbino.

The atlas depicts cities which neither Marco nor the geographers know exist or where they are, though they cannot be missing among the forms of possible cities: a Cuzco on a radial and multipartite plan which reflects the perfect order of its trade, a verdant Mexico on the lake dominated by Montezuma's palace, a Novgorod with bulb-shaped domes, a Lhassa whose white roofs rise over the cloudy roof of the world. For these, too, Marco says a name, no matter which, and suggests a route to reach them. It is known that names of places change as many times as there are foreign languages; and that every place can be reached from other places, by the most various roads and routes, by those who ride, or drive, or row, or fly.

"I think you recognize cities better on the atlas than when you visit them in person," the emperor says to Marco, snapping the volume shut.

And Polo answers, "Traveling, you realize that differences are lost: each city takes to resembling all cities, places exchange their form, order, distances, a shapeless dust cloud invades the continents. Your atlas preserves the differences intact: that assortment of qualities which are like the letters in a name."

The Great Khan owns an atlas in which are gathered the maps of all the cities: those whose walls rest on solid foundations, those which fell in ruins and were swallowed up by the sand, those that will exist one day and in whose place now only hares' holes gape.

Marco Polo leafs through the pages; he recognizes Jericho, Ur, Carthage, he points to the landing at the mouth of the Scamander where the Achaean ships waited for ten years to take the besiegers back on board, until the horse nailed together by Ulysses was dragged by windlasses through the Scaean gates. But speaking of Troy, he happened to give the city the form of Constantinople and foresee the siege which Mohammed would lay for long months until, astute as Ulysses, he had his ships drawn at night up the streams from the Bosporus to the Golden Horn, skirting Pera and Galata. And from the mixture of those two cities a third emerged, which might be called San Francisco and which spans the Golden Gate and the bay with long, light bridges and sends open trams climbing its steep streets, and which might blossom as capital of the Pacific a millennium hence, after the long siege of three hundred years that would lead the races of the yellow and the black and the red to fuse with the surviving descendants of the whites in an empire more vast than the Great Khan's.

The atlas has these qualities: it reveals the form of cities that do not yet have a form or a name. There is the city in the shape of Amsterdam, a semicircle facing north, with concentric canals—the princes', the emperor's, the nobles';

there is the city in the shape of York, set among the high moors, walled, bristling with towers; there is the city in the shape of New Amsterdam known also as New York, crammed with towers of glass and steel on an oblong island between two rivers, with streets like deep canals, all of them straight, except Broadway.

The catalogue of forms is endless: until every shape has found its city, new cities will continue to be born. When the forms exhaust their variety and come apart, the end of cities begins. In the last pages of the atlas there is an outpouring of networks without beginning or end, cities in the shape of Los Angeles, in the shape of Kyōto-Ōsaka, without shape.

Cities & the Dead · 5

Like Laudomia, every city has at its side another city whose inhabitants are called by the same names: it is the Laudomia of the dead, the cemetery. But Laudomia's special faculty is that of being not only double, but triple; it comprehends, in short, a third Laudomia, the city of the unborn.

The properties of the double city are well known. The more the Laudomia of the living becomes crowded and expanded, the more the expanse of tombs increases beyond the walls. The streets of the Laudomia of the dead are just wide enough to allow the gravedigger's cart to pass, and many windowless buildings look out on them; but the pattern of the streets and the arrangement of the dwellings repeat those of the living Laudomia, and in both, families are more and more crowded together, in compartments crammed one above the other. On fine afternoons the living population pays a visit to the dead and they decipher their own names on their stone slabs: like the city of the living, this other city communicates a history of toil, anger, illusions, emotions; only here all has become necessary, divorced from chance, categorized, set in order. And to feel sure of itself, the living Laudomia has to seek in the Laudomia of the dead the explanation of itself, even at the risk of finding more there, or less: explanations for more than one Laudomia, for different cities that could have been and were not, or reasons that are incomplete, contradictory, disappointing.

Rightly, Laudomia assigns an equally vast residence to those who are still to be born. Naturally the space is not in proportion to their number, which is presumably infinite, but since the area is empty, surrounded by an architecture all niches and bays and grooves, and since the unborn can be imagined of any size, big as mice or silkworms or ants or ants' eggs, there is nothing against imagining them erect or crouching on every object or bracket that juts from the walls, on every capital or plinth, lined up or dispersed, intent on the concerns of their future life, and so you can contemplate in a marble vein all Laudomia of a hundred or a thousand years hence, crowded with multitudes in clothing never seen before, all in eggplant-colored barracans, for example, or with turkey feathers on their turbans, and you can recognize your own descendants and those of other families, friendly or hostile, of debtors and creditors, continuing their affairs, revenges, marrying for love or for money. The living of Laudomia frequent the house of the unborn to interrogate them: footsteps echo beneath the hollow domes; the questions are asked in silence; and it is always about themselves that the living ask, not about those who are to come. One man is concerned with leaving behind him an illustrious reputation, another wants his shame to be forgotten; all would like to follow the thread of their own actions' consequences; but the more they sharpen their eyes, the less they can discern a continuous line; the future inhabitants of Laudomia seem like dots, grains of dust, detached from any before or after.

The Laudomia of the unborn does not transmit, like the city of the dead, any sense of security to the inhabitants of the living Laudomia: only alarm. In the end, the visitors' thoughts find two paths open before them, and there is no telling which harbors more anguish: either you must think that the number of the unborn is far greater than the total of all the living and all the dead, and then in every pore of the stone there are invisible hordes, jammed on the funnel-sides as in the stands of a stadium, and since with each generation Laudomia's descendants are multiplied, every funnel contains hundreds of other funnels each with millions of persons who are to be born, thrusting their necks out and opening their mouths to escape suffocation. Or else you think that Laudomia, too, will disappear, no telling when, and all its citizens with it; in other words the generations will follow one another until they reach a certain number and will then go no further. Then the Laudomia of the dead and that of the unborn are like the two bulbs of an hourglass which is not turned over; each passage between birth and death is a grain of sand that passes the neck, and there will be a last inhabitant of Laudomia born, a last grain to fall, which is now at the top of the pile, waiting.

Cities & the Sky · 4

Summoned to lay down the rules for the foundation of Perinthia, the astronomers established the place and the day according to the position of the stars; they drew the intersecting lines of the decumanus and the cardo, the first oriented to the passage of the sun and the other like the axis on which the heavens turn. They divided the map according to the twelve houses of the zodiac so that each temple and each neighborhood would receive the proper influence of the favoring constellations; they fixed the point in the walls where gates should be cut, foreseeing how each would frame an eclipse of the moon in the next thousand years. Perinthia—they guaranteed—would reflect the harmony of the firmament; nature's reason and the gods' benevolence would shape the inhabitants' destinies.

Following the astronomers' calculations precisely, Perinthia was constructed; various peoples came to populate it; the first generation born in Perinthia began to grow within its walls; and these citizens reached the age to marry and have children.

In Perinthia's streets and square today you encounter cripples, dwarfs, hunchbacks, obese men, bearded women. But the worse cannot be seen; guttural howls are heard from cellars and lofts, where families hide children with three heads or with six legs.

Perinthia's astronomers are faced with a difficult choice. Either they must admit that all their calculations were wrong and their figures are unable to describe the heavens, or else they must reveal that the order of the gods is reflected exactly in the city of monsters.

Continuous Cities · 3

Each year in the course of my travels I stop at Procopia and take lodgings in the same room in the same inn. Ever since the first time I have lingered to contemplate the landscape to be seen by raising the curtain at the window: a ditch, a bridge, a little wall, a medlar, a field of corn, a bramble patch with blackberries, a chicken yard, the yellow hump of a hill, a white cloud, a stretch of blue sky shaped like a trapeze. The first time I am sure there was no one to be seen; it was only the following year that, at a movement among the leaves, I could discern a round, flat face, gnawing on an ear of corn. A year later there were three of them on the wall, and at my return I saw six, seated in a row, with their hands on their knees and some medlars in a dish. Each year, as soon as I entered the room, I raised the curtain and counted more faces: sixteen, including those down in the ditch; twenty-nine, of whom eight were perched in the medlar; forty-seven, besides those in the chicken house. They look alike, they seem polite, they have freckles on their cheeks, they smile, some have lips stained by blackberries. Soon I saw the whole bridge filled with round-faced characters, huddled, because they had no more room to move in; they chomped the kernels of corn, then they gnawed on the ears.

And so, as year followed year, I saw the ditch

vanish, the tree, the bramble patch, hidden by hedges of calm smiles, between round cheeks, moving, chewing leaves. You have no idea how many people can be contained in a confined space like that little field of corn, especially when they are seated, hugging their knees, motionless. They must have been many more than they seemed: I saw the hump of the hill become covered with a thicker and thicker crowd; but now that the ones on the bridge have got into the habit of straddling one another's shoulders, my gaze can no longer reach that far.

This year, finally, as I raise the curtain, the window frames only an expanse of faces: from one corner to the other, at all levels and all distances, those round, motionless, entirely flat faces are seen, with a hint of a smile, and in their midst, many hands, grasping the shoulders of those in front. Even the sky has disappeared. I might as well leave the window.

Not that it is easy for me to move. There are twenty-six of us lodged in my room: to shift my feet I have to disturb those crouching on the floor, I force my way among the knees of those seated on the chest of drawers and the elbows of those taking turns leaning on the bed: all very polite people, luckily.

Hidden Cities · 2

In Raissa, life is not happy. People wring their hands as they walk in the streets, curse the crying children, lean on the railings over the river and press their fists to their temples. In the morning you wake from one bad dream and another begins. At the workbenches where, every moment, you hit your finger with a hammer or prick it with a needle, or over the columns of figures all awry in the ledgers of merchants and bankers, or at the rows of empty glasses on the zinc counters of the wineshops, the bent heads at least conceal the general grim gaze. Inside the houses it is worse, and you do not have to enter to learn this: in the summer the windows resound with quarrels and broken dishes.

And yet, in Raissa, at every moment there is a child in a window who laughs seeing a dog that has jumped on a shed to bite into a piece of polenta dropped by a stonemason who has shouted from the top of the scaffolding, "Darling, let me dip into it," to a young serving-maid who holds up a dish of ragout under the pergola, happy to serve it to the umbrella-maker who is celebrating a successful transaction, a white lace parasol bought to display at the races by a great lady in love with an officer who has smiled at her taking the last jump, happy man, and still happier his horse, flying over the obstacles, seeing a francolin flying in the sky, happy bird freed from its cage by a painter happy at having painted it feather by feather, speckled with red and yellow in the illumination of that page in the volume where the philosopher says: "Also in Raissa, city of sadness, there runs an invisible thread that binds one living being to another for a moment, then unravels, then is stretched again between moving points as it draws new and rapid patterns so that at every second the unhappy city contains a happy city unaware of its own existence."

Cities & the Sky · 5

Andria was built so artfully that its every street follows a planet's orbit, and the buildings and the places of community life repeat the order of the constellations and the position of the most luminous stars: Antares, Alpheratz, Capricorn, the Cepheids. The city's calendar is so regulated that jobs and offices and ceremonies are arranged in a map corresponding to the firmament on that date: and thus the days on earth and the nights in the sky reflect each other.

Though it is painstakingly regimented, the city's life flows calmly like the motion of the celestial bodies and it acquires the inevitability of phenomena not subject to human caprice. In praising Andria's citizens for their productive industry and their spiritual ease, I was led to say: I can well understand how you, feeling yourselves part of an unchanging heaven, cogs in a meticulous clockwork, take care not to make the slightest change in your city and your habits. Andria is the only city I know where it is best to remain motionless in time.

They looked at one another dumbfounded. "But why? Whoever said such a thing?" And they led me to visit a suspended street recently opened over a bamboo grove, a shadow-theater under construction in the place of the municipal kennels, now moved to the pavilions of the former lazaretto, abolished when

the last plague victims were cured, and—just inau-
gurated—a river port, a statue of Thales, a toboggan
slide.

"And these innovations do not disturb your city's
astral rhythm?" I asked.

"Our city and the sky correspond so perfectly,"
they answered, "that any change in Andria involves
some novelty among the stars." The astronomers,
after each change takes place in Andria, peer into
their telescopes and report a nova's explosion, or a
remote point in the firmament's change of color from
orange to yellow, the expansion of a nebula, the
bending of a spiral of the Milky Way. Each change
implies a sequence of other changes, in Andria as
among the stars: the city and the sky never remain
the same.

As for the character of Andria's inhabitants, two
virtues are worth mentioning: self-confidence and
prudence. Convinced that every innovation in the
city influences the sky's pattern, before taking any
decision they calculate the risks and advantages for
themselves and for the city and for all worlds.

Continuous Cities · 4

You reproach me because each of my stories takes you right into the heart of a city without telling you of the space that stretches between one city and the other, whether it is covered by seas, or fields of rye, larch forests, swamps. I will answer you with a story.

In the streets of Cecilia, an illustrious city, I met once a goatherd, driving a tinkling flock along the walls.

"Man blessed by heaven," he asked me, stopping, "can you tell me the name of the city in which we are?"

"May the gods accompany you!" I cried. "How can you fail to recognize the illustrious city of Cecilia?"

"Bear with me," that man answered. "I am a wandering herdsman. Sometimes my goats and I have to pass through cities; but we are unable to distinguish them. Ask me the names of the grazing lands: I know them all, the Meadow between the Cliffs, the Green Slope, the Shadowed Grass. Cities have no name for me: they are places without leaves, separating one pasture from another, and where the goats are frightened at street corners and scatter. The dog and I run to keep the flock together."

"I am the opposite of you," I said. "I recognize only cities and cannot distinguish what is outside them. In uninhabited places each stone and each clump of grass mingles, in my eyes, with every other stone and clump."

Many years have gone by since then; I have known many more cities and I have crossed continents. One day I was walking among rows of identical houses; I was lost. I asked a passerby: "May the immortals protect you, can you tell me where we are?"

"In Cecilia, worse luck!" he answered. "We have been wandering through its streets, my goats and I, for an age, and we cannot find our way out. . . ."

I recognized him, despite his long white beard; it was the same herdsman of long before. He was followed by a few, mangy goats, which did not even stink, they were so reduced to skin-and-bones. They cropped wastepaper in the rubbish bins.

"That cannot be!" I shouted. "I, too, entered a city, I cannot remember when, and since then I have gone on, deeper and deeper into its streets. But how have I managed to arrive where you say, when I was in another city, far far away from Cecilia, and I have not yet left it?"

"The places have mingled," the goatherd said. "Cecilia is everywhere. Here, once upon a time, there must have been the Meadow of the Low Sage. My goats recognize the grass on the traffic island."

Hidden Cities · 3

A sibyl, questioned about Marozia's fate, said: "I see two cities: one of the rat, one of the swallow."

This was the interpretation of the oracle: today Marozia is a city where all run through leaden passages like packs of rats who tear from one another's teeth the leftovers which fall from the teeth of the most voracious ones; but a new century is about to begin in which all the inhabitants of Marozia will fly like swallows in the summer sky, calling one another as in a game, showing off, their wings still, as they swoop, clearing the air of mosquitos and gnats.

"It is time for the century of the rat to end and the century of the swallow to begin," the more determined said. In fact, already beneath the grim and petty rattish dominion, you could sense, among the less obvious people a pondering, the preparation of a swallowlike flight, heading for the transparent air with a deft flick of the tail, then tracing with their wings' blade the curve of an opening horizon.

I have come back to Marozia after many years: for some time the sibyl's prophecy is considered to have come true; the old century is dead and buried, the new is at its climax. The city has surely changed, and perhaps for the better. But the wings I have seen moving about are those of suspicious umbrellas under which heavy eyelids are lowered; there are people who believe they are flying, but it is already an achievement if they can get off the ground flapping their batlike overcoats.

It also happens that, if you move along Marozia's compact walls, when you least expect it, you see a crack open and a different city appear. Then, an instant later, it has already vanished. Perhaps everything lies in knowing what words to speak, what actions to perform, and in what order and rhythm; or else someone's gaze, answer, gesture is enough; it is enough for someone to do something for the sheer pleasure of doing it, and for his pleasure to become the pleasure of others: at that moment, all spaces change, all heights, distances; the city is transfigured, becomes crystalline, transparent as a dragonfly. But everything must happen as if by chance, without attaching too much importance to it, without insisting that you are performing a decisive operation, remembering clearly that any moment the old Marozia will return and solder its ceiling of stone, cobwebs, and mold over all heads.

Was the oracle mistaken? Not necessarily. I interpret it in this way: Marozia consists of two cities, the rat's and the swallow's; both change with time, but their relationship does not change; the second is the one about to free itself from the first.

Continuous Cities · 5

To tell you about Penthesilea I should begin by describing the entrance to the city. You, no doubt, imagine seeing a girdle of walls rising from the dusty plain as you slowly approach the gate, guarded by customs men who are already casting oblique glances at your bundles. Until you have reached it you are outside it; you pass beneath an archway and you find yourself within the city; its compact thickness surrounds you; carved in its stone there is a pattern that will be revealed to you if you follow its jagged outline.

If this is what you believe, you are wrong: Penthesilea is different. You advance for hours and it is not clear to you whether you are already in the city's midst or still outside it. Like a lake with low shores lost in swamps, so Penthesilea spreads for miles around, a soupy city diluted in the plain; pale buildings back to back in mangy fields, among plank fences and corrugated-iron sheds. Every now and then at the edges of the street a cluster of constructions with shallow facades, very tall or very low, like a snaggle-toothed comb, seems to indicate that from there the city's texture will thicken. But you continue and you find instead other vague spaces, then a rusty suburb of workshops and warehouses, a cemetery, a carnival with Ferris wheel, a shambles; you start down a street of scrawny shops which fades amid patches of leprous countryside.

If you ask the people you meet, "Where is Penthesilea?" they make a broad gesture which may mean "Here," or else "Farther on," or "All around you," or even "In the opposite direction."

"I mean the city," you ask, insistently.

"We come here every morning to work," someone answers, while others say, "We come back here at night to sleep."

"But the city where people live?" you ask.

"It must be that way," they say, and some raise their arms obliquely toward an aggregation of opaque polyhedrons on the horizon, while others indicate, behind you, the specter of other spires.

"Then I've gone past it without realizing it?"

"No, try going on straight ahead."

And so you continue, passing from outskirts to outskirts, and the time comes to leave Penthesilea. You ask for the road out of the city; you pass again the string of scattered suburbs like a freckled pigmentation; night falls; windows come alight, here more concentrated, sparser there.

You have given up trying to understand whether, hidden in some sac or wrinkle of these dilapidated surroundings there exists a Penthesilea the visitor can recognize and remember, or whether Penthesilea is only the outskirts of itself. The question that now begins to gnaw at your mind is more anguished: outside Penthesilea does an outside exist? Or, no matter how far you go from the city, will you only pass from one limbo to another, never managing to leave it?

Recurrent invasions racked the city of Theodora in the centuries of its history; no sooner was one enemy routed than another gained strength and threatened the survival of the inhabitants. When the sky was cleared of condors, they had to face the propagation of serpents; the spiders' extermination allowed the flies to multiply into a black swarm; the victory over the termites left the city at the mercy of the wood-worms. One by one the species incompatible to the city had to succumb and were extinguished. By dint of ripping away scales and carapaces, tearing off ely-tra and feathers, the people gave Theodora the exclu-sive image of human city that still distinguishes it.

But first, for many long years, it was uncertain whether or not the final victory would not go to the last species left to fight man's possession of the city: the rats. From each generation of rodents that the people managed to exterminate, the few surviviors gave birth to a tougher progeny, invulnerable to traps and resistant to all poison. In the space of a few weeks, the sewers of Theodora were repopulated with hordes of spreading rats. At last, with an extreme massacre, the murderous, versatile ingenuity of man-kind defeated the overweening life-force of the enemy.

The city, great cemetery of the animal kingdom, was closed, aseptic, over the final buried corpses with their last fleas and their last germs. Man had finally reestablished the order of the world which he had himself upset: no other living species existed to cast any doubts. To recall what had been fauna, Theodora's library would preserve on its shelves the volumes of Buffon and Linnaeus.

At least that is what Theodora's inhabitants believed, far from imagining that a forgotten fauna was stirring from its lethargy. Relegated for long eras to remote hiding places, ever since it had been deposed by the system of nonextinct species, the other fauna was coming back to the light from the library's basements where the incunabula were kept; it was leaping from the capitals and drainpipes, perching at the sleepers' bedside. Sphinxes, griffons, chimeras, dragons, hircocervi, harpies, hydras, unicorns, basilisks were resuming possession of their city.

Hidden Cities · 5

I should not tell you of Berenice, the unjust city, which crowns with triglyphs, abaci, metopes the gears of its meat-grinding machines (the men assigned to polishing, when they raise their chins over the balustrades and contemplate the atria, stairways, porticos, feel even more imprisoned and short of stature). Instead, I should tell you of the hidden Berenice, the city of the just, handling makeshift materials in the shadowy rooms behind the shops and beneath the stairs, linking a network of wires and pipes and pulleys and pistons and counterweights that infiltrates like a climbing plant among the great cogged wheels (when they jam, a subdued ticking gives warning that a new precision mechanism is governing the city). Instead of describing to you the perfumed pools of the baths where the unjust of Berenice recline and weave their intrigues with rotund eloquence and observe with a proprietary eye the rotund flesh of the bathing odalisques, I should say to you how the just, always cautious to evade the spying sycophants and the Janizaries' mass arrests, recognize one another by their way of speaking, especially their pronunciation of commas and parentheses; from their habits which remain austere and innocent, avoiding complicated and nervous moods; from their sober but tasty cuisine, which evokes an ancient golden age: rice and celery soup, boiled beans, fried squash flowers.

From these data it is possible to deduce an image of the future Berenice, which will bring you closer to knowing the truth than any other information about the city as it is seen today. You must nevertheless bear in mind what I am about to say to you: in the seed of the city of the just, a malignant seed is hidden, in its turn: the certainty and pride of being in the right—and of being more just than many others who call themselves more just than the just. This seed ferments in bitterness, rivalry, resentment; and the natural desire of revenge on the unjust is colored by a yearning to be in their place and to act as they do. Another unjust city, though different from the first, is digging out its space within the double sheath of the unjust and just Berenices.

Having said this, I do not wish your eyes to catch a distorted image, so I must draw your attention to an intrinsic quality of this unjust city germinating secretly inside the secret just city: and this is the possible awakening—as if in an excited opening of windows—of a later love for justice, not yet subjected to rules, capable of reassembling a city still more just than it was before it became the vessel of injustice. But if you peer deeper into this new germ of justice you can discern a tiny spot that is spreading like the mounting tendency to impose what is just through what is unjust, and perhaps this is the germ of an immense metropolis. . . .

From my words you will have reached the conclusion that the real Berenice is a temporal succession of different cities, alternately just and unjust. But what I wanted to warn you about is something else: all the future Berenices are already present in this instant, wrapped one within the other, confined, crammed, inextricable.

The Great Khan's atlas contains also the maps of the promised lands visited in thought but not yet discovered or founded: New Atlantis, Utopia, the City of the Sun, Oceana, Tamoé, New Harmony, New Lanark, Icaria.

Kublai asked Marco: "You, who go about exploring and who see signs, can tell me toward which of these futures the favoring winds are driving us."

"For these ports I could not draw a route on the map or set a date for the landing. At times all I need is a brief glimpse, an opening in the midst of an incongruous landscape, a glint of lights in the fog, the dialogue of two passersby meeting in the crowd, and I think that, setting out from there, I will put together, piece by piece, the perfect city, made of fragments mixed with the rest, of instants separated by intervals, of signals one sends out, not knowing who receives them. If I tell you that the city toward which my journey tends is discontinuous in space and time, now scattered, now more condensed, you must not believe the search for it can stop. Perhaps while we speak, it is rising, scattered, within the confines of your empire; you can hunt for it, but only in the way I have said."

Already the Great Khan was leafing through his atlas, over the maps of the cities that menace in nightmares and maledictions: Enoch, Babylon, Yahooland, Butua, Brave New World.

He said: "It is all useless, if the last landing place can only be the infernal city, and it is there that, in ever-narrowing circles, the current is drawing us."

And Polo said: "The inferno of the living is not something that will be; if there is one, it is what is already here, the inferno where we live every day, that we form by being together. There are two ways to escape suffering it. The first is easy for many: accept the inferno and become such a part of it that you can no longer see it. The second is risky and demands constant vigilance and apprehension: seek and learn to recognize who and what, in the midst of the inferno, are not inferno, then make them endure, give them space."